WHITE BUFFALO
WOMAN

Dolores Richardson

Order this book online at www.trafford.com
or email orders@trafford.com

Most Trafford titles are also available at major online book retailers.

Printed in the United States of America.

ISBN: 978-1-4669-2220-4 (sc)
ISBN: 978-1-4669-2221-1 (hc)
ISBN: 978-1-4669-2222-8 (e)

Library of Congress Control Number: 2012905601

Trafford rev. 03/26/2012

 www.trafford.com

North America & international
toll-free: 1 888 232 4444 (USA & Canada)
phone: 250 383 6864 ♦ fax: 812 355 4082

CONTENTS

her. One brave cuts a large piece out of
her red curls and pins it in his hair. Then
one of them picks her up and carries her
to their camp. She ends up in the death
house where she's led out by another white
girl. While crawling to get away, they stop
to rest. A man in Cavalry uniform kills
the girl who helped Jane. He picks Jane
up. And walks to the campfire where the
others are sitting and drinking. .... 89 thru 96

CHAPTER 1

Outside the orphanage, a storm raged through the City of London. The wind screeched and whistled as it loosened rooftop slates and dislodged flower pots from their usual doorway moorings. Rain clattered on the cobblestone streets sounding much like marbles hitting the glass windows of the building. Thunder boomed and lightning lit up the sky.

Inside Bethany Orphanage for Destitute Children, the children in the Dormitory whimpered and cried occasional quiet sobs as if trying not to attract the storm's notice. Children crawled into bed with other children so they would not have to listen to the shattering noises alone. Some of them whispered their prayers. Others hummed softly. A few were so frightened they remained totally still and unmoving.

Down the hall, the Nursery stood empty, devoid of children under the age of three. Its door yawned open like a cavity admitting all the world to view its deserted bassinettes and cradles. That is, until something, maybe it was the noises from the storm outside caused the door to slam shut. Then, perhaps because of a lock being turned open there began a back and forth movement of opening and closing. "BAM-BOP" sounded the door as it opened and then closed with a bang. "BAM-BOP" was just enough to startle not only the whimpering children in the Dormitory, but also Mrs. Adelaide Grimm, Supervisor and Administrator of the Orphanage that she referred to as "BODC" for Bethany Orphanage for Destitute Children.

Mrs. Grimm's room was downstairs on the first floor near her Office. From that location all she could hear besides the screeching winds was the "BAM-BOP, BAM-BOP" of the door of the Nursery. She crawled into her bed and pulled the covers up and over her head to shut out the noise.

1

Upstairs, down the hall from the Nursery and the Dormitory rooms, Marcy Ann, Ruby, and Esther were shivering in their beds, praying for protection, not in the least remembering the frightened children they had been hired as child care workers to look after and keep safe.

Marcy Ann, tall and bone thin at age forty-seven, was promising God that she would never stick her tongue out at ugly people anymore if only God would make the storm stop.

Ruby, soft and plump with thinning hair at age twenty-five, was repeating over and over for God to have mercy on her soul, have mercy on her soul, have mercy on her soul. She said it so many times it had begun to sound like "Od ha mersee un me sul." She wondered if the sound of it could carry over the storm, or even if God would notice.

Esther, with waist long ash brown hair in two braids at age eighteen, shivered. Even her tongue was shivering between her clenched teeth. She just knew they were all dying, or would die. She dared the lightning to pierce her in her heart, Then she dared it to stop its flashing in the high window of the room and light up in her head. Thunder sounded with a BOOM, and then a CRACK CRACK CRACK followed. She wondered about her best friend, Dorothy and she immediately challenged the storm to kill them both. "Go ahead," she hissed into the crackling air, "Kill us all, I dare you. Kill me. Kill Dorothy. I dare you." As if she could back the weather down with a challenge.

Dorothy, whose room was across the hall from Esther, was writing in her diary, "This morning at 5:15 A.M. London time, October 10, 1838, my baby girl was born. She is perfect all over. Every inch of her is so beautiful, from her heart-shaped face with its dot of an upturned nose, pink bow lips, jade green eyes, coral colored hair all tightly curling around her head. And all the way down her peachy white body, tiny hands clenching and opening, down to her legs which will one day stretch straight and strong. Then on down to her feet and delicately formed toes. Thank You, God, for such a miracle! I have waited so long to . . . . " There the writing stopped. Like a long trail the ink dripped in a gash straight down the page as Dorothy's hand held on, trying, so it seemed, to stay straight across instead of down the page.

With a long sigh, Dorothy Jean Perkins exhaled from way deep inside her being and slid halfway to the floor off the bed. There she remained with hands holding fast. There is where she was found later after the storm had ended. By then, it was 7:05 A.M. and the stiffness of rigor mortis had set in so that one hand was still holding to the thick comforter on her bed while the other was holding the book.

Esther knocked, and then opened the door to Dorothy's room. She gasped at the sight of her friend sprawled half on the floor in a pool of blood and half on the bed with her hands still holding to the bedspread, to the book. She could not take in what her eyes were seeing. She gasped again. She heard the mewing from the bundle beyond Dorothy's hands. She wondered how a cat got into the building. She looked closer to see the diary. She read its last entry, words that refused to sink in. Gingerly Esther reached over to pull the corner of the soft flannel from the baby's face. She gasped a third time, and then breathed, "A baby . . . . " How could there be a baby?

Esther looked down onto the top of her friend's chestnut hair, so soft and shiny, spread across her snowy face, her eyes blankly staring . . . . focused . . . . set, her mouth softly curved up into a half smile as if appreciating some private knowing not available to anyone else.

Esther shivered harder than she had during the storm. For one crazy minute, Esther believed her challenge for the lightning to kill Dorothy had worked. She wondered why it had not killed her as well. They had promised to share everything.

Both Dorothy and Esther had longed to be free of the work, the demanding Mrs. Grimm, the sad squalling children, the loneliness of never having strong arms caress and hold you. They had felt a kinship. They had become close as sisters. Both had promised what happened to one would happen to the other.

Then jealousy and wonder stirred Esther. Dorothy HAD experienced enough freedom to get pregnant. Dorothy HAD known what it was to be caressed and held. Esther gasped again. She would never have guessed that about her friend. Then, stepping backwards, Esther's leg accidentally touched Dorothy's dead body and its rock hardness jolted her into reality.

Esther jumped backwards again and went flying down the hall screaming for all to hear, "A baby, Dorothy's had a baby, Dorothy's dead." All the way down the hall, then down the stairs. Then past the surly cook holding a spatula who was exiting Mrs. Grimm's room, and on through the open door where Mrs. Grimm stood holding her nightgown up to her abundant bosom. "Dorothy's had a baby." Esther announced matter of factly. "Dorothy is dead."

There was palpable silence in the room. Mrs. Grimm seemed to hold her breath while reaching for her clothes, not able to mix together what she was hearing with what she was thinking and feeling. Perhaps not wanting the worker girl, Esther, to see her shameful nakedness so fresh from the cook's porky hands.

Then just as suddenly, Adelaide Grimm came to herself and, eyeing Esther, she announced. "Well, thank you for interrupting my morning even further after that hideous storm! Get back upstairs and tend the baby. Or go to your work. Or whatever it is you're supposed to be doing." She paused as if to determine what Esther ought to be doing. "Tend the children as you should," she dictated further, finally sounding more like herself. "Do just leave the body, uh . . . or bodies, whatever, for the doctor." She looked straight at Esther who was still looking at her. She took a step forward then after she was fully clothed. "Get out of here, girl, and do your work! Now! Now! Go on!" She shook her hand as if dismissing the whole thing.

Esther did as she was told. She left Mrs. Grimm's room and slammed the door behind her. She became aware then of her heart beating, of her veins throbbing, of the blood coursing through her young healthy body. Finally, she was beginning to feel alive again. She was not dead, thank God, like poor Dorothy. Then guilt set in for feeling such relief.

As she walked slowly back up the stairs, Esther remembered the pungent smell. She wondered how she could look at Dorothy again kneeling in all that blood. She wondered if she herself might ever be in such danger, and even whether every woman who had a baby was in such danger. Esther vowed never to get pregnant herself if that was so. Oh, but how awful it would be never to feel a man's embrace. Oh, it was just too horrible to think about. Suddenly, like a banshee encircled by its enemies, Esther laughed a twisted, stinging laugh. She knew she would not do it like Dorothy had anyway. No indeed. No indeed. No.

Esther walked on by past Marcy Ann and Ruby who were sobbing, wailing aloud. Both of them were standing there staring into Dorothy's room. Esther walked straight to the bed and picked up the coral haired baby girl and turned to leave the room again. Then she seemed to have another thought, and she turned and picked up the diary from off the bed, snatching it loose from one of Dorothy's frozen hands. She slammed the diary in a drawer of Dorothy's dresser and turned to leave. "Do not DARE touch that book," she warned Marcy Ann and Ruby as she noted the look of horror on their faces, with their tears still streaming. "It's evidence!" Then she added with disgust. "You two look a mess. Straighten up before Mrs. Grimm discharges you both."

Then Esther walked to the Nursery, she kicked the broken door open, and she stood there wondering which cradle or crib to put her down in. Poor little thing, with no mother or father, would it even matter?

Meanwhile, downstairs, Adelaide Grimm was instructing Tom Parsifal, the driver, to fetch Dr. Rogers to come and pronounce the dead body and look over the new baby. Tom nodded and drove the horse and buggy to the doctor's house and brought him back. When returned with the good doctor, Tom stayed close as he could to find out the whole story. He knew, with luck and the right facts, he could take the information to a man he knew who was a reporter and maybe he could make a shilling or more. But the good doctor refused to allow Tom to accompany him upstairs. Tom slipped up anyway.

On the climb up the stairs, Adelaide Grimm complained incessantly about the inconvenience of the storm, of suddenly "finding out this way" that one of her child care workers was pregnant, and of having another baby to feed and take care of, "As if we are made of money!" she had exclaimed to Dr. Rogers.

Streaks of red shot across Percy's face as he continued to listen to the droning litany being spewed by Mrs. Grimm. Money was all she ever worried about. Not poor Dorothy who felt pressed enough to hide her pregnancy from everyone and then died giving birth. Not the poor baby who now was encribbed in an unwelcome place.

As they reached the top of the stairs and turned toward Dorothy's room, Percy's heart pounded in his chest just remembering Dorothy's cream-colored skin, full breasts and lemony-flavored lips. He remembered how eagerly he had folded her in his arms. And how willing she had been to allow him in her room. He hoped she was not as they had described her to him. Then a tremor grabbed him from head to foot as if to shake his remorse, sift his heart's motives. When he turned to step into Dorothy's room, his heart stopped at the sight that awaited him. The seventeen-year-old girl he had held in gentle embrace only once, he now realized had paid an awful price for her disrobing.

A loud gasp escaped his lips. Adelaide Grimm stared up at him. Tom, who was skulking outside Dorothy's door hugging the wall to stay out of the doctor's sight, thrust his head around to see what caused the doctor's reaction.

Red streaks grew darker on Percy's face and neck. He made himself walk over to the body. He reminded himself that Dorothy no longer inhabited it. Then he reached to touch her hand, and felt it stony hard, as cold as marble. It was dry, not warm and soft anymore. He could not pry her fingers loose from the comforter, so he stopped trying. Perspiration soaked his collar. His hands started shaking. He lifted one hand then to dismiss all those who were with him. "Get out, all of you!" he warned them, "This is not going to be a pleasant sight!"

He did not realize he was standing on sticky floor until he turned and his feet flew out from under him. He landed with his head near Dorothy's stockinged foot. He jumped up grunting and gasping like he had been wounded. He remembered kissing that lavender-smelling foot. He had adored every soft curve of her voluptuous body.

In that dead weight of a moment, he could not believe he would be able to turn that body over to anyone else to prepare it for its proper rest. How could he allow an embalmer to take a knife and render it into a cadaver?

A loud roar came up from somewhere deep inside Percy and exploded into Adelaide Grimm's face. "Get yourself away from Dorothy, out of this room" Then he shook all over like a tornado had grabbed hold inside him. "Let me do my job!" He said over and over. "Let me do my job!"

They all backed out one by one. Tom had heard enough. He had his facts, information enough for a story, and he went straight to the reporter friend of his. He got five shillings for it, too. He felt fine about it.

Percy had participated in many autopsies. He had viewed countless dead bodies. At age fifty-seven, he had a long practice behind him. No dead body was a mystery to him, and yet he wished Dorothy's was. He had a pervasive feeling that he did not, would not, could not allow anyone else to touch her. He bathed her body. He dressed it. He closed her eyes. He wept. He had communion. He cried her death song. He begged forgiveness.

When he finished with the body, he mopped away the blood as well as he could using the same pan Dorothy had used earlier for the birth. Her blood stains still showed visibly on his suit jacket and pants where he'd fallen earlier. The smell of blood in his nostrils was acrid and sickeningly sweet at the same time.

His grief finding a hidden place deep within him, he opened the door and called for Adelaide to "Send for the porters to remove the girl's body." He filled out the Certificate of Death. The quill scratched noisily as he drew in the words for the cause: ABNORMAL LOSS OF BLOOD, HEMORRHAGE AT CHILDBIRTH.

He knew that if he had been there with her, she would have been alive even then. She would have been suckling their child at this very moment.

With that thought, he suddenly stood and went directly to the Nursery, past the broken door still swinging back and forth sounding its "BAM-BOP" sound. He walked over to the crib where the little bundle lay mewing soft crying sounds. He pulled aside the tightly coiled blanket. As he looked at her, he began to fill with unashamed joy from his feet to his head. He placed his hands on her curly coral hair and rubbed ever so gently down the entire surface of her soft, peachy body, feeling her tiny warm fingers, her delicate bone structure, the soft warmness, on down the gently curving legs and tiny feet and toes. He looked carefully at her abdomen and noted a precisely formed umbilical knot. He could not have done it any better himself! He saw she was perfect from head to toe. Then he looked into her heart-shaped face, into her sparkling jade eyes, and he whispered, "Oh, my daughter! Then he wept.

Dr. Percy Rogers picked up the naked little girl and held her high as if performing some ancient ritual to the gods. In the turmoil of his raging mind, in the twisting of his mourning heart, he pledged to heaven and to Dorothy that he would care for this little one the rest of his life. Then he dressed her, he wrapped her warmly in blankets, and he gave her a bottle. He waited patiently while she learned to suck in the life sustaining liquid. He then took her downstairs and informed Adelaide Grimm that he would take the child home to Agnes where they would discuss adoption.

Adelaide, still chafing over the doctor having rudely ordered her out of Dorothy's room (it was more HER room than Dorothy's) earlier, merely looked at him as if he had lost his mind by snatching that baby up as he had and then taking it home. "Humph!" was all Mrs. Grimm replied. She was left muttering under her breath to herself. "He's probably the real father anyway, him with his high-handed ways, always expecting Dorothy to come right with him on his rounds, just as if he was the King of England. Indeed!" But, as she thought more about it, her anger mellowed. If he adopted the baby, then he would be obliged to pay a sum, and every penny was needed by BODC. The whole situation could turn out for their benefit. Finally, she had to turn her attention to the funeral arrangements, a pauper's funeral of course, with the girl, Dorothy, having no relatives that anyone knew about. Adelaide sniffed and then started making plans.

Esther had tried to catch up with Dr. Rogers but he had left too suddenly while she was upstairs with one of the children in the dormitory. Esther had the diary in her pocket. She had wanted to offer it to the doctor. "Oh, well." Esther thought to herself as she looked out the front door of the building. "Maybe I could read it first after all!" Then she went back upstairs to finish rounding up the children for their midday meal.

Percy had hoped for a warm reception when he came into the house with the baby. Agnes surprised him. She took one look at the baby with hair so like his own and then went running upstairs to her room. When he asked to talk to her about adoption, she refused. She insisted she would have nothing to do with any child but their own. Percy knew she must be aware that was not a likelihood. With her fifty-second birthday very near, she was past child-bearing age. "For a good and kind woman, Agnes, you do have some rather annoying blind sides." Percy told her carefully.

"Perhaps," Agnes had replied to Percy. "But not nearly as blind as you to even suggest that we adopt an orphan whose parents you know absolutely nothing about. Her mother could have been a loose woman, and her father a murderer for all you know. Think what an awful creature that child could grow up to be!" For Agnes, that was the end of it.

Percy had to accept defeat. He decided he would plan for a later victory. He left Agnes and went to his study. He took a Certificate of Birth from his desk drawer and began to fill in the information for Dorothy's baby. He looked over at the sleeping infant he had placed in his big chair. Then he looked down and began to write in bold letters, JANE ANN PERKINS. Then he filled in the date, OCTOBER 10, 1838, and the approximate time of birth. He wrote after Mother DOROTHY JEAN PERKINS, and after the word Father he hesitated while thinking to himself how everything would change dramatically if he did admit the truth. If he wrote "Rogers" then Jane Ann would be protected. Yet, he might lose Agnes whom he loved dearly. His own reputation as a doctor might be tarnished. Then, without further thought, Percy scratched after Father UNKNOWN. After Place of Birth, he wrote Bethany Orphanage for Destitute Children. He cursed himself for losing courage at the last minute. He knew he should have put his name on the certificate as Father. He knew he ought to have put ROGERS for Jane Ann's last name.

As he walked to the window and looked out at the Autumn flowers blooming in the Gardens, he wondered how he would ever be able to keep his promise to care for the child if he had to take her back to Bethany Orphanage.

CHAPTER 2

Thousands of miles away from London, in the far reaches of the territory of the Teton Sioux "Lakota" peoples in the northwest of America, the winter of 1838 was already bringing great hardship to the people. The snows were deep for October. Crazy Dog had gathered the Crow children and Grandfather the Sioux children, and taken them to a cave deep in the Black Hills. They made a big campfire and started telling stories about their people. Among the dozen or so children who came with them were Sixteen-year-old Red Cloud, eight-year-old Rain and six-year-old Bear Claw. As the heavy snow kept on falling, the mothers and old people came into the cave with them until the place was warm enough from all the heat of the bodies and the joyful anticipation on the people's faces as they listened to Crazy Dog and Grandfather.

"Long ago, after a big snow storm just like this," Crazy Dog nodded toward the white haze of falling ice crystals, "the hearts of the people grew dark and weary from loss of hope. They lost their vision. No one cried out to the Great Spirit anymore. Everyone began to look at their brothers and sisters with thoughts that "This one means me harm" or "This one wants my goods." As a result, the families began to break apart and the people separated and moved away from each other. Finally the snows stopped and the air cleared enough that the young warriors could go out hunting." Crazy Dog moved around the circle of eager faces as he spoke. His voice filled the air and made it warmer.

"There were three of the young men who chose to go together to see if they could find enough elk or rabbit or wild turkeys to keep their families from starving. While they were walking in the clearing near the Pa Sapa here, they saw a very beautiful girl walking toward them. The oldest fell in love at first sight and he told his friends how he felt, but they cautioned him to wait and hear what the girl had to say. When they got up close to her, they saw she was even more beautiful than any girl they had ever seen. She wore a soft white buckskin dress and moccasins. She had green and red shiny stones decorating the hem and the sleeves and neck. Even on her moccasins. Every time the sun flashed off one of the stones, the young men were more helpless and under her spell." Crazy Dog watched Red Cloud inch his way closer through the younger ones. This was his favorite part.

"The girl asked where they were going and the young men told her they were out hunting for their people. She turned and pointed to the Black Hills and told them all that they needed to live could be found there. Great herds of buffalo were in the canyons. And horses enough to last a whole lifetime. They could get as many lodge poles as they needed from the trees every time they moved back in this area to hunt. When they were not too hungry, they could find deer and mountain goats and elk for their fires, as well as prairie chickens. Then when they wanted to praise the Creator for giving them all these good things, they could go into the mountains and cry from the hills, and their voices would always be heard."

Bear Claw smiled as he thought of hearing these words from a girl. He looked over at his friends, Red Cloud and Rain, but they were staring at Crazy Dog, waiting for the rest of the story.

"The girl told them more things than this." Crazy Dog continued. "When she was through talking, she waved to them and turned to walk away. As they watched her, she rolled over to the East and then she rolled over to the West. She rolled in all four directions while the young hunters stood there watching her. When she stood up again, she told them they should keep the Peace Pipe in a safe place in one of the caves in Pa Sapa. She told them all the people should meet together every year and smoke the Pipe in all four directions. In this way, the people will always live in peace. And, all the people and the Great Spirit will remain connected as one." He stopped and stared into the fire for a long time. If they were not in the cave but outside in the open, at this time Crazy Dog would have thrown some of the black dust in the fire and made a small explosion to wake them up to the important part. This time, he just stared at the fire hoping the movement of the flames would impress the truth into their minds.

Bear Claw stood up to ask Crazy Dog a question. When Crazy Dog nodded to him to speak, Bear asked, "Can we go hunting now and find this lady?" But a few around the fire snickered as if he asked a stupid question.

"This is a good thing to ask, Bear Claw," Crazy Dog's answer surprised all those who had hoped to make fun of him. "If White Buffalo Woman can come one time when the people need her wisdom, then she can come another time. Do you believe that?"

Bear nodded yes and saw that all the others were nodding, too. "Then, I want to go hunting and find White Buffalo Woman and give peace and plenty back to our people. I don't want my father to die fighting the Pawnee or Cheyenne warriors. Or maybe out hunting for provisions. I want him to be with me always."

Crazy Dog nodded. All the children were joining in with Bear Claw some saying they wanted to go with him as soon as the snow was over. Red Cloud, too, was nodding that he would go with them. Grandfather watched them. He knew that Red Cloud wanted to count a lot of coup first before he became a peacemaker. He thought of how he could show them instead of telling them what was important in the story.

Grandfather looked around and spied a basket with fruit in it that one thoughtful mother had brought in for the children. He walked close to her and bent and whispered and she handed him the basket. He strolled back to the group and, taking a handful of berries, he passed them around first to the right and then to the left. "Each one of you take one berry, wait until I say eat, then put it in your mouth." When he saw everyone in the circle had a berry in hand, he said, "Eat." They all chewed and when he gave them time to swallow, he asked, "Is the berry gone?" Some said yes, some no. "Is it dead because you can no longer see it or hold it?" he questioned further. Some nodded no, some yes. "Can you remember what it felt like in your hand? What it tasted like in your mouth?" Everyone nodded. He motioned to Rain to answer the next question. "What happens to the berry that you swallowed?"

"Part of the berry goes through our body keeping us healthy and strong. The part the body cannot use goes out into the earth where it becomes nourishment again for the soil and for other tiny creatures."

Red Cloud raised his hand to ask a question. Grandfather nodded. "If nothing living is ever lost then, why is killing wrong sometimes?" Red Cloud asked them.

Crazy Dog smiled and asked, "Why did you eat the berry?"

Red Cloud thought about that for a minute while looking for the trick answer. "I ate the berry because you told me to." Immediately Red Cloud flushed and wished he had not said it, even wished he'd said anything else.

Crazy Dog smiled. "That is a good answer, Red Cloud. That is the reason most of the killing goes on. Somebody says go kill my enemy with me. When I do, then that man and his people become my enemy, too, and the enemy of my people."

"Is it wrong to kill?" Red Cloud countered.

"When we kill an animal to feed ourselves and our loves ones, do we not pray to the Great Spirit and ask forgiveness of that animal and all its relatives?"

The winter storm had quieted by then. All the young children were deep in thought and both Crazy Dog and Grandfather knew they would be talking together and figuring out the right answers. It had been a good gathering.

CHAPTER 3

At age three, Jane Ann was sent with the other children on the wagon, with Mr. Parsifal driving them all to work each day. Jane Ann was a delightful three-year old. Esther, Ruby, and Marcy Ann all loved her. She was so pretty with her red hair, thick and curly, falling in ringlets all down her back. Her body was thin and perfectly proportioned. Her face was heart-shaped and her nose was a perfect shape and size, with her lips like tiny rosebuds as pink as could be Her complexion was pale, almost like the finest of porcelain, flawlessly beautiful. She had tiny little feet and hands. Ruby often told her, "You have hands for clapping and feet for dancing." With that invitation Jane Ann would begin tapping her feet and jumping all around, that is, until they heard Mrs. Grimm's "Ah-hum!"

Jane Ann loved the sun and begged to be out in the sunshine every day. Sunlight had always been an occasional rarity in London, and almost everyone would go out when it was a clear day. It seemed especially important to the younger children. One of the ladies would take Jane Ann and the other little girls out to play and they would run and laugh and have such a glorious time!

That ended abruptly when Jane Ann was three years old and Mr. Parsifal announced, "C'mon ye little doggerels let us be on our way to Pennyworth's." He usually had a handful of sweets which he would pass out one at a time into the hands of those who were walking too slow or wanting to stay behind. "C'mon, let's rush it now!" he would call, and off they would go.

But Jane Ann would often stamp her foot. "I don't like it," she would cry, "I want to go back to Mrs. Grimm's NOW!"

The other children knew she would not get her way. Each of them had protested the same thing in one way or another. Not a one of them wanted to spend a moment in the dingy dark factory room. Most of them protested as Jane Ann was doing. Each of them had been punished and then made to sit at the long table bench where they would find themselves sitting for long periods of time from then on. Occasionally one of them would put up a fuss but it was short-lived. There was no place else to go. No one to turn to, no one even to tell or to talk to about it. Mr. Parsifal wouldn't listen. The ladies at the Orphanage were afraid to listen, except in secret whispers of sympathy, for they all needed to work. It would have taken a very brave child to attempt to talk to Mrs. Grimm about it. But there was one who had.

Nine-year old Jeremy Tharpe had told Mrs. Grimm one time that they were mistreated and should not be punished so much at the factory. She had punished him yet again by sending him to his room after a nine-hour work day and only a biscuit to eat, with no supper at all. Later, when he was heard crying, she had Mr. Parsifal go up and whip him.

Jane Ann persisted though, time and again, trying for months to make the supervisor, Elmore Scruggs, take them back to the Orphanage or else let them go outside. He refused with a firm, "No, absolutely NO!" He would take her by the arm and drag her to her chair, set her down, and put her hands on the thimbles.

Pennyworth's sold different colored thimbles and Jane Ann's job was to separate them by color and put them in different boxes. Mr. Scruggs had complained about Jane Ann's short attention span before. Now it seemed to be getting worse. He, too, could see the sun's rays shining through the filthy window. He wondered if these pesky children could only know how much he, too, longed to be out in the sun.

There was a window located high up from the floor so as not to give anyone the idea they could go outside when they wished. It was propped open by two long poles that were hooked to two very substantial-appearing hooks just below the window. The sun streamed in, scattering its rays a little here and there. Usually the room was so dark and dreary that the children would sit working slowly, not seeming to have much energy, while some grumbled aloud about being hungry, or having to go to the bathroom, or anything. On this day, most of the children just looked longingly at the sunshine or the rays of sunlight that they could see splashing in from high above.

Jane Ann had been forced back into her seat three times already and it was not lunch time yet. At lunch time, if they had not caused a ruckus or complained or made Mr. Scruggs punish them more than three times, they would get a piece of brown bread and a cup of lukewarm tea for lunch.

"You have your limit now, young lady!" Mr. Scruggs warned her in his screeching voice. "One more time and you will have no bread and tea!"

Tears slid down her cheeks but she did not cry out loud. She just wanted to see the sunlight just one time! She determined with all her might that she would climb up to that window and look out. Oh, if only they had a door, then she could walk to it and look out! But there was only the high up window. Jane Ann had never tried to climb up that high before, but she knew she could do it somehow.

As soon as Elmore Scruggs went to the office to get his papers or some more trays of work for the children (they were not sure which) Jane Ann made her move. She piled some boxes on top of each other and quickly climbed up. She reached one of the pegs in the wall and made her way as quickly as she could to reach the hooks that were propping up the poles that kept the window open. Just as she reached it, the big hook pulled out of the wall and the rod came banging down on Jane Ann's head. The window plopped down also hitting Jane Ann on the head. She fell in a heap on top of the boxes, probably the only thing that saved her life.

Elmore Scruggs came running back into the work area. Some of the children were trying to get Jane Ann off the boxes. "Wait, don't touch her," Elmore screamed. "She could be dead." The children pulled back in horror. Some of them started crying and bawling. Jeremy had already reached her and he was lifting her off the crumpled boxes.

Elmore stared at her and leaned down. He could feel faint breathing so she was still alive! "Come on," he motioned to Jeremy, "Bring her on." He went as fast as he could, leading Jeremy who was holding Jane Ann out to where Mr. Parsifal lay asleep in the wagon. "Get up and take us to Dr. Rogers' address immediately!" He called.

Mr. Parsifal did as he was told. He popped the whip so the horses would move faster through the street. They almost flew to Dr. Rogers' office. "Is she alive?" Mr. Parsifal questioned Elmore.

Mr. Scruggs could only nod. He guessed she was. He didn't want to touch her. This would not be the first child to die because of being in the factory. But he didn't want to think about that at all either.

Agnes Rogers heard the sound of a wagon pulling up in front of the house and she met them at the door. She was horrified to see the limp body of a little girl being carried by a boy who was obviously undernourished. She recognized Mr. Parsifal as the driver at Bethany Orphanage. She did not know Elmore Scruggs. It was Elmore who was explaining what had happened, and not explaining it well at all.

"He wasn't even in the room when she fell," Jeremy said quietly.

Agnes smiled at him and nodded. "Alright gentlemen, both of you wait out in the sitting room if you please." She held her hand up when Mr. Parsifal reached to pull Jeremy with them. "The boy will help me fetch the doctor. Leave him!" And Mr. Parsifal shrugged and did as he was told.

When they had closed the door behind them, she turned to Jeremy. "Quickly now and as clearly as you can, please tell me what happened."

He told her about Jane Ann climbing up to the window to see the sunlight better, and about the hook flying out of the wall, "and then," he continued, "she was hit by the rod and then the window, kerblam! She just crumpled up like a rag doll and fell to the boxes and smashed them." He paused, and then, "Lucky those boxes just crumpled. If she had hit her head on that hard floor, she'd be a smashed pumpkin herself!" He shook his head.

Agnes had Jane Ann covered with a soft blanket, and she was holding her arm feeling for a pulse. "Young man," she stated.

"I'm Jeremy Tharpe, I'm at the Orphanage where Jane Ann is."

"Jeremy," Agnes said kindly, "Go upstairs please to the second room on the left and you will see Dr. Rogers. Ask him to come here and tell him what you've told me, please."

Jeremy nodded and did as he was told. The men he came with were now sitting in the Waiting Room. They looked at him as if he was daft when he walked through. They nodded at him. Jeremy was doing exactly as he was told.

Dr. Rogers was sitting in his easy chair. Jeremy knocked on the door. He quickly explained what was happening downstairs and that the Misses "needs you to come, please," and they both walked swiftly down the stairs.

Jeremy sat down in the same room with Mr. Scruggs and Mr. Parsifal. After a few minutes quiet, Jeremy smelled sweet rolls and his stomach lurched. He had not been given anything to eat since the dry bread and watery tea yesterday at noon. He was very hungry. His stomach growled. He wondered if he could ask for a bite.

The maid brought a tray of sweet bread and a pot of tea with cups for everyone. Mr. Parsifal hurried up and reached for a bread. "No," the woman snapped. "Not until Misses Agnes gives you leave to eat." Then she looked at the boy who was obviously in some discomfort. "The lad though, he can have a bread and a cup of tea. You are grown men, you can wait." Both men looked angry but they remained speechless. They just sat and watched Jeremy gulp down two or three breads and a whole cup of tea. The maid stood there as if to make sure they left the boy alone.

When Dr. Rogers came out, he asked which one was from the factory and Elmore Scruggs stepped up. "You may return to the factory, with our gratitude for getting the girl here so fast. She is in grave danger. She will not go back with you." He stopped Elmore from saying anything. "Get your bread and tea and go ahead with it back to your factory."

Then he turned to Mr. Parsifal. "You are Parsifal, right?" He nodded and Mr. Parsifal gulped, he sure wanted one of those breads, too. "You return Mr. Scruggs here to his factory, then return to Mrs. Grimm at the Orphanage. Tell her for me that the girl may not live. She is to stay here until she expires or else gets better. Do you understand me?" Mr. Parsifal nodded his head up and down. "Take this note of explanation to her, please."

"As for you, young man, you are a hero," Dr. Rogers said to Jeremy. "You shall be recommended for some other work than where you are, someplace like a bakery or a shop, somewhere your quick thinking will be appreciated." He paused and watched the boy swallow. "Go ahead, take your time and eat all you want."

"Oh, Parsifal," he called as Mr. Parsifal was going out. "The lad will stay here with us also for a time. Tell Mrs. Grimm when she has found suitable placement for him in some work more suited, such as a bakery or a store or even a newspaper, then she is to let me know and I will see he gets back his clothes and such. Just tell her . . . . oh, never mind! I will tell her myself. Just tell her I kept him here with us because of having saved the little girl's life. Do you understand?

Mr. Parsifal nodded his head up and down. He had a mouthful of bread so he could not answer outright. (Mrs. Grimm favored the doc so she wouldn't give himself a hard time for leaving the boy there. But it made him wonder why the doc was being so particular with them two. A softie no doubt. Mrs. Grimm would probably wonder about that, too, him taking so much on himself and all.)

When Jane Ann's head was sutured and she was resting peacefully, they moved her upstairs to one of the patient bedrooms. They called Tillie, one of the maids, to come in and sit and watch her. That would be her job all night.

"If she comes around, ring that bell or send the boy to fetch me, alright?" Dr. Rogers told Tillie. Then turning to the boy, he asked, "What is your name, boy?"

"Jeremy Tharpe, sir," the boy answered.

The doctor smiled and nodded. "Find yourself a pillow, lad, and sleep there on the floor. You are to help Tillie listen out for the little girl."

Later, in their own room, as they were going to sleep, Percy and Agnes talked about what had happened. "Of course, the girl will stay here. We cannot send her back to that awful place!" Agnes said, "And that wonderful little boy, if we send him back, they will starve him!"

"Alright, dear, we will keep them both for awhile anyway. They cannot take Jane Ann away because she is hurt too bad, but Mrs. Grimm may send for the boy." Percy warned Agnes.

"You can keep them from taking BOTH of them! I know you can." Agnes had pleaded.

"Sh.h.h. We have to figure out how hurt she is. She took a bad bang there on her head in two places. It may be that she will never wake up. Then again, little children are very resilient. We will just wait and see." Then he added. "You might remember her in your prayers, my dear." And then they both finally went to sleep.

Down the hall, sleeping on a pallet in Jane Ann's room, Jeremy felt like he had died and gone to paradise! His stomach was full of bread and tea. His friend, the little girl, Jane Ann, was still sleeping. He prayed to God that she would be alright.

CHAPTER 4

PLOP PLOP Jane Ann woke hearing a strange plopping sound. A lady sat beside her bed with her head leaning sideways, and she appeared to be sound asleep in her chair. Occasionally a soft WOOO sound could be heard coming from the lady's mouth as she exhaled. But that was not where the PLOP PLOP sound was coming from! Jane Ann's head was hurting but not as much as when she first fell. Then Jane Ann began to wonder where she was. Nothing around her was familiar.

"Oh," she heard herself say as she moved around to get a better look.

"Say" a familiar voice called, and Jeremy's head came up from the floor at the foot of her bed. "Are you awake, Jane Ann?" Sure enough, it was Jeremy!

Jane Ann laughed and said, "I'm so glad to see you."

The sleeping lady woke up, too. "Goodness, young lady," she began, being somewhat embarrassed that she had fallen asleep while watching the poor little thing. "How are you doing, little one?" She woke all the way and began fluttering around. Then she settled into a chuckle. "My, I must have been napping, some nurse I am! I will go and tell the good doctor you are awake."

"The doctor?" Jane Ann wondered aloud. "Where am I? Where is Grimm and Esther and, Jeremy? She turned to look at the foot of her bed. "Where are we?"

The lady cautioned both children to shush and sit quietly until she returned, and then she left the room.

After the door closed, Jane Ann attempted to sit up and lean her feet off the bed.

Jeremy came around to the side of her bed and sat in the same chair the woman had. "That's Tillie," he said nodding toward the door where the lady just left. Then, "Janie I'm so glad you are going to be alright! You gave me such a scare! Bonkers, you gave us all a big scare!." Jeremy was looking at her from head to foot it seemed. "You fell from the window," Jeremy reminded her, "at Pennyworth's, do ye remember now? Scruggs was scared to death you had been killed but I felt you still had breath and I picked you up in me arms. Mr. Parsifal, oh you should have seen him, Jane Ann, the doctor put him in his place, and Scruggs, too." Jeremy was talking so fast and laughing at the same time.

Jane Ann kept up with him though. "I remember now about falling. But that's all I remember." Then, "Are we going home to Grimm's?" Jane asked him quietly. "Sh.h.h.h, don't even suggest that out loud! We do not want to go back there. Remember, you are very hurt and sick, and we have to stay here. Just go along with it, and let's not ever go back to Grimm's!" Jeremy was urging her when the door opened.

Dr. Rogers, Agnes, and the maid, Tillie, came into Jane Ann's room. "Well, well, Let's see how you are today, little Jane Ann." Dr. Rogers said as he was entering Jane Ann's room. He turned and patted Jeremy on the head. "I see you're still watching over your little friend, and that's good, Jeremy."

Jane Ann watched the three of them. Dr. Rogers felt and listened and moved her arms and legs this way and that way very gently. She could hear Mrs. Agnes telling Tillie what to bring up for the two children to eat. She could see Tillie nodding.

"Well, Missy," Dr. Rogers ended his examination, "You are not going to be very active for awhile, but I believe you will heal up nicely. You are a very lucky young girl, and you have your friend, Jeremy, here to thank for saving your life. The man, Scruggs, would have left you lie on the floor at the factory probably from now on, but young Jeremy picked you up and started to bring you by himself to us!"

Jeremy smiled dutifully even though he thought the doctor was praising him far too much.

Jane Ann smiled and nodded. Suddenly, she began to feel very sleepy again.

The doctor noticed her eyes closing and opening. "Don't worry, you just sleep when you want. The medicine we're giving you will cause you to be sleepy. Your head will also want you to sleep more while it is healing. You just doze and wake when you please until very soon you shall be feeling fine and well." He patted her little arm. She was such a lovely little girl, and he was very glad he had named her after his own Mother. After all, Jane Ann was a fine name and it fit this little one perfectly.

"You surely do look as if you belong here with us, Janie," Agnes said smiling. She was trying to make sure the girl felt at ease and not uncomfortable with her new surroundings. Yet she could not help but notice the similarity in Percy's and the girl's head of hair. That brick-red hair was, after all, a Rogers' family trademark. Now she decided it must belong to other families as well. "Such pretty red hair!" Then, "I am so glad you are beginning to wake up. Tell Jeremy or Tillie if there is anything you want us to bring you. And, please, stay as still as you can until you are all healed!" She could see the little one was having a time keeping her eyes open.

After the doctor and Agnes had left, Jane asked sleepily, "What was making the plop plop sound, Jeremy?"

Jeremy patted her hand and, turning it over, he put a little rubber ball in it. "Here girl, I was bouncing this off the end of your bed hoping to get you to wake up and let me know you are alright, and it worked!" His voice seemed to Jane Ann to be getting farther and farther away. "Now," Jeremy continued, "you hold onto it and we will play ball lots outside in the sun when your head is all healed up."

Jane Ann drifted into sleep again listening to Jeremy and thinking of the sunshine outside and of playing ball with Jeremy.

Another two weeks had passed before Jane Ann was awake for any length of time. Dr. Rogers had been sure to give her plenty of time to get over the fall, to be as sure as possible that nothing further was going to come from her head injury. Actually, he knew it could be months before she fully recovered. He did not intend for her, or the boy, Jeremy, to go back to the Orphanage.

Percy decided finally to call his lawyer at Dudley, Dudley and Fitch, who advised him to petition for temporary custody without rights to inheritance for the children, of course, for both of the children.

Mrs. Grimm tried to argue Dr. Rogers out of his decision to be custodian of the two children. It was, after all, money cheated from the

Orphanage and there were many children who might suffer because of it. That was her way of thinking about it until Percy reminded her that he donated his time free each month to tend all the children as well as the staff at Bethany Orphanage. His time and medical expertise should be worth something to her and the Orphanage. At that point, Percy won the disagreement over rights, and he, Agnes and Mrs. Grimm tried to make the best of what could have been a disagreeable situation.

For both Jane Ann and Jeremy, the situation was wonderful. Neither child had ever had quite "enough" good food to eat. Neither had ever been able to sleep late or to play in the sunshine outside at will. Jeremy gloried in his new found freedom and he found just having three meals a day a real treat! He hoped they never returned to Grimm's authority. Never!

Jane Ann continued to heal up nicely from her accident. However, for many months she continued to have excruciating headaches which would last an hour or so and then suddenly stop. At those times, she would go to her room and close the door only to come out later happy and appearing to feel very well.

Christmas time came and the children enjoyed having presents for the first time. Percy was delighted that Agnes favored the children for she and Percy still had no child of their own. Although she did not wish to discuss actually being their Mother, yet she informally had already taken on that role. Daily she tutored Jeremy and began to teach Jane Ann to read. She found both children had very fine minds. Jane delighted in being read to, and also in learning to write her name.

At the end of the year, Mrs. Grimm asked for Jeremy's return. "Just one of the children will help us immensely," she had pleaded with Percy, "as we are so lacking in money that our children are going hungry!" As if having one more child to put out for wages would make a difference.

Agnes, however, was upset at the thought. She had become very fond of Jeremy. As a result, she set out again speaking to women's committees in even more earnest, and they were able to raise enough money to quiet Mrs. Grimm for a time.

Agnes began to fear the money situation would reappear periodically as long as the children were around. Therefore, she and Percy spoke to a relative who managed a newspaper and asked if he would take on Jeremy as a paid apprentice. After he spoke with Jeremy, he agreed to have the boy apprentice with his paper, and part of that apprenticeship was a stipend that would be paid to Jeremy's parent (he had none) or to his guardian. At that point, Percy had his lawyer draw up papers giving Mrs. Grimm and the Orphanage guardianship of Jeremy again, with the stipulation that Jeremy finish his apprenticeship. The Orphanage would get the stipend which meant that Jeremy would continue earning money regularly for them. It freed Jeremy, at least of starvation and overwork. Agnes and Percy trusted her cousin to be fair with the boy. And he would live there at the boarding house and not at the Orphanage. So it had finally been agreed upon amiably for all! The Orphanage had a regular income because of Jeremy, and Mrs. Grimm was pleased. Jeremy may have been the most pleased of all!

Jane Ann was not as happy. She was fond of Jeremy as a sister for a brother, and it was hard for a four year old to just say goodbye and never see him again. Then Agnes and Percy reassured Jane Ann and Jeremy that him living at the boarding house and working his apprenticeship at the newspaper didn't have to mean a break in their family. He would continue to visit regularly, as well as to visit and spend holidays with them.

"Now, Jane Ann," Agnes was saying, "We have helped Jeremy and now we must keep you safe from ever going back to that horrid place!" Agnes promised to find a way to prevent that happening. "My dear, where on earth did you get such thick and beautiful hair?" Agnes laughed again as the brush continued to tangle in Jane Ann's mass of curls.

Jane Ann giggled. The girls at the Orphanage had always said the same thing when they brushed her hair there. "I don't know! I don't know!" Jane Ann would answer. She answered Agnes now, "I don't know where it came from." And "The ladies at Grimm's told me my Mama didn't have red hair, she had brown, and I must have got it from some other relative!"

Percy could hear them just outside the door, as he walked in to say goodnight to Jane Ann. Both Agnes and Jane Ann looked up to see Percy's massive head of red curly hair. Jane Ann pointed, "See, Doctor Percy has red hair just like mine."

For the first time, Agnes really allowed herself to see and accept the likeness. Of course, she had noticed it before, but now she really looked and thought about it. Percy had never mentioned the likeness of the hair and name with that of his Mother, yet Agnes was thinking, Jane Ann was exactly his own Mother's name! Also, the child bore a striking resemblance to the women of the Rogers' family. Agnes almost asked Percy about it at that moment, but for some reason unknown to her, she did not. Later, maybe she would. For now Agnes did not want to spoil the moment. Each day she could pretend Jane Ann was theirs, only pretend, for she still felt that she could not adopt anyone else's child as her own. Someday though, she was determined, she would give Percy a red haired little girl or boy. With that thought, Agnes lay aside all her doubts. She was just as determined to enjoy Jane Ann's time with them and to pretend she was their daughter!

The days and months passed into years. Jeremy was found to be fond of his work at the printing office of the newspaper, as well as his room and board at the rooming house. He was already 14 years old when Jane Ann was 5. He had become interested in finishing his studies and he hoped to become a writer. He and Jane Ann began to grow apart.

Although Jane Ann was sad when Jeremy would be invited over to the Rogers' house for the holidays and not come. It seemed to Jane Ann that he never came to play ball with her or to sit on the porch reading as they had at first. The older the children grew, the less Jane Ann was able to cling to Jeremy. She, too, had other children to play with, other little girls and young gentlemen more her age. However, when Jeremy did come, it was to Jane Ann's delight because it was only he who knew about the spirit people who came to talk with her when she had a headache.

It was Jeremy who told Percy and Agnes about the "people" Jane Ann saw when she had headaches. It was quite by accident one Christmas that just as Jeremy was getting ready to go back to the newspaper flat at the boarding house where he lived, Jane Ann had grabbed him in a big hug, "Please don't stay away so long," she had pleaded.

"Oh, Janie," Jeremy had said, "I'm sorry that I almost forgot to ask you how your headaches have been?" Then in front of the doctor and his wife, without (perhaps) any forethought at all, Jeremy asked her, "Do the people still appear and talk to you when you have the headaches?" She wondered if he had forgotten this was their "secret?"

Jane Ann had blushed and she was hoping Dr. Percy and Ms. Agnes did not hear Jeremy's question. She whispered in a low but rather stern voice, "Goodnight!" all the while shaking her head as if to let him know NOT to repeat the question.

Both Percy and Agnes had heard Jeremy's question, and Percy spoke up. "What about seeing and hearing people, Jane Ann? Is this true?"

She shook her head vigorously. "It was way back when I first started having the headaches. Now I do not, not really, anymore." She did not want to talk to them about it. "Goodbye, Jeremy, see you next time." Jane Ann called, and then she turned to go to her room.

Tillie stopped her on the stairs for a hug. "Child, how could you know I wanted that package of thimbles? I really do like my present, and I thank you so much."

Jane Ann nodded and hugged her in return. As she looked over Tillie's shoulder, she could see Percy and Agnes watching, both of them with puzzled looks on their faces. She hoped they would forget about the "people", and perhaps they had already forgotten. She certainly hoped so.

In early Spring of her ninth year, Jane Ann was on the screened veranda with her easel and paints. Agnes had been so delighted with the drawings she had found Jane Ann doing that she called in a tutor who could teach Jane Ann how to use paints and water colors. It had been with charcoal that she excelled "like an accomplished artist" the tutor had exclaimed.

Jane Ann had thrived with the lessons. Having the big paper to draw on was such fun, and the weather was so nice, except for the misty rain. However, Jane Ann even loved the rain.

That day on the porch, she was drawing on the paper, concentrating so hard that she hardly heard the screen door open and the two people walk in. They may have stood behind her several minutes in silence, not wanting to break the artist's moment, when suddenly the man gasped, "Look there, Emma, that looks like Mother!"

"Yes, she's even wearing the frock we gave her to wear at the last dinner party we attended together. Oh, my, this is the best drawing I've seen of anyone!" Emma said.

Jane Ann was startled for a moment and then she gave a wide smile. "Hello, my name is Jane Ann, are you here to see the doctor?"

The couple smiled at each other. The man answered first. "My dear," he said to Jane Ann, "I believe I am here to see you as well as my good brother, the doctor, and his lovely wife, Agnes."

Then the woman said, "I am Emma, and I wonder how you can know my mother in-law so very well! You are a fine artist to be such a young

26

girl!" Emma gushed on about the dress, the woman in the drawing, all of which was a puzzle to Jane Ann.

The woman's red hair was very much like Jane Ann's own. "Look," Emma continued talking, "Look there at her lovely red curls, so much like yours and Percy's and your dear departed Mother's. Look, this is so uncanny, so fascinating." Emma could not stop herself. She was a real talker when she was happy. Right then she felt very happy!

By this time, Agnes and Percy and Tillie had all come onto the porch and hugs started going on all around. Tillie was patting Jane Ann on the arm and whispering, "Finally, Jane Ann, you get to meet the fun side of the family. You will adore them both."

Jane Ann was thinking that she already did adore the whole family. She loved Percy and Agnes, and now she loved her Uncle Harold and Aunt Emma as well. However, she could not understand why they were so surprised about her drawing of the lady, until she remembered they did not know about the spirit people talking to her. None of them knew she had ever seen her! This sweet lady had been talking to her and encouraging her every time she had a headache to leave her scribbles and drawings where Agnes could see them. Because of that, Mrs. Agnes had given her plenty of drawing materials and paper. And, most important, she'd brought in a teacher who gave Jane Ann lots of praise, something she really needed, along with her lessons.

Percy smiled as he looked at the drawing of his Mother.

Agnes breathed a long sigh. "Percy, that . . . . that's your Mother!" Agnes said.

"Yes," Percy agreed with a nod.

Harold joined in. "And a grand and talented rendition of our beautiful Mother, I would say, too." Then he put his hand on Jane Ann's shoulder. "It's beautiful, Jane Ann."

"It's a little younger than we remember her perhaps," Emma smiled, "but just as beautiful as she really was when she was well." Emma pulled Jane Ann's hand, and started dancing around with her.

Percy wondered how in the world Jane Ann could know their Mother. She had never seen her. She had died four years before Jane Ann was even born! He began to wonder really what was going on.

They all recovered from surprise enough to welcome Harold and Emma in to make themselves at home for their visit. Tillie started rushing around to get the table ready. Percy and Agnes both continued to wonder about the drawing Jane Ann had done. Where had she heard such details about the red haired Mother of Percy and Harold? Also, how would she know what her clothes looked like or how she liked her hair? It was a real mystery and Harold and Emma loved a mystery. Not one of them could entirely forget the millions of questions that one drawing had brought to mind.

Jane Ann had always been bright, inquisitive, and eager to learn. At nine, her favorite place in the Rogers' household had been the library. Whenever she came up missing, she could be found in the library reading another book. Percy observed her love of reading and, in an effort to widen her knowledge of the world to include more than medicine and Agnes's beloved love novels (almost the entirety of the Rogers' Library), he presented her on her tenth birthday with a book of her own entitled, "Journals of Wislizenus." It was written by a German man who had gone to America and traveled through the South Platte area in the great plains where some Indian peoples had lived for a long time. These Indian peoples were a favorite of Jane Ann's. When asked how they could be her favorite, she replied that, "Look here, they're talking about the Lady who talks to me sometimes." Percy had thought she meant in her dreams then.

CHAPTER 5

Everyone was so busy over the next weeks that hardly anyone had time to talk at length with Jane Ann or, in particular, to question her about her drawing of Mother Rogers. Actually, when they did discuss the odd coincidence with her drawing tutor, he had simply suggested that they wait until the drawing was finished. So, Percy and Harold had waited anxiously for her to finish that one. Only Percy, and later Esther at the Orphanage, had known that it was the good doctor who had named Dorothy's baby Jane Ann. He hesitated to speak about it at the present time because it might pain Agnes should he have to tell the whole story about who Jane Ann's real father was. Certainly, he did not want to send Jane Ann back to the Orphanage! This must never happen.

At dinner one evening, the idea of parentage came up and Harold talked about it outright. The drawing of Mother Rogers had just been finished as a beautiful painting and then hung ceremoniously in the large dining room in a place of honor. Jane Ann had been pleased. Now they were at the table, the two men and two ladies, with Jane Ann finished eating and having gone up to her room after dinner.

Harold said, "Percy, if you and Agnes had not adopted Jane Ann, we would have for sure!" He was looking at Emma who was nodding in agreement.

Agnes interrupted him, "But we haven't formally adopted her yet. I had always rather wanted to wait to have our own child." She hurried on to explain. "Jane Ann is a dear girl an I would not dream of her having to go back to that Orphanage, I'm sure it's horrid. Then she turned to Percy. "She won't have to, will she Percy?"

"No, dear, not back to the Orphanage certainly. You see, Harold," Percy said turning to his brother, "Our attorney drew up an agreement of guardianship which, of course denies her any inheritance rights, but does grant us the privilege of having her live here with us." He paused.

Harold was shocked. "Inheritance rights, none? You would deny the girl any security? Suppose we all should die and leave her alone. This could be the most absurd thing I've heard lately. My own brother denying an innocent but gifted girl any monies to pursue her talent should anything happen to him. What on earth are you thinking?

Emma shook her head as if unable to believe Percy would be so parsimonious.

Percy did not quite know what to say. If he and Harold were alone, he would have told the whole truth of the matter at that moment, but the ladies were still at the table. "Ha-rumph!" Percy cleared his throat. "I am taking good care of the girl, as you will notice, and she has a home here with us just as if she is our daughter." He turned to Agnes to allow her to say how she felt.

Agnes just shook her head. She would be hard pressed to explain just how she loved Jane Ann, and she did care for her, but she did not want exactly to claim her.

"We did not then, and we do not now want her to return to the Orphanage." Percy wanted to make that clear. "This artistic talent she has, well, I do not understand how she could have drawn our Mother, I truly do not."

Harold hit his pipe on the side of his cup. "Drat that Orphanage, this is an angel of a girl anyone would be proud to call daughter!" Then he looked at Emma. "How about Emma and me as parents?" (Emma was nodding 'yes'.) You see, Percy and Agnes, we do want to be her father and mother. We do want to rear her and watch her enormous talent grow and grow. We do not give a fig how she knows what our Mother looked like. See here," Harold was trying to tone down his enthusiasm some. We love the child. We have loved her since first sight as a matter of fact, even before we saw the painting of Mother." He paused then and looked over at Emma and smiled.

"Yes, yes!" Emma enthusiastically agreed. "If her talents are going to blossom, she certainly needs stability."

Agnes knew this might happen! Harold and Emma were always like that, gregarious, immediate, driven by impulse, not the least like Percy and herself who thought everything through thoroughly first, detail by detail, before making any decision. She suspected they would never understand how she felt about the girl. She was thinking how much she loved her.

"Adopt her then. We can all love her." Percy found himself saying. In the back of his mind he was thinking that one day he had to tell Harold the whole story about Jane Ann. Harold would not even mind! Percy knew that. Then looking at Emma's ecstatic face, he knew she would not mind either.

Percy continued to explain. "Her mother was a childcare worker at the Orphanage with no relatives anyone knows of, and I don't believe anyone would even block you from adopting her." At that point, he thought of Mrs. Grimm and her whining insistence about money for the Orphanage. Yet he also knew a few shillings enough would stop her disapproval.

As it turned out, it was easier than any of them thought. Mrs. Grimm was happy to have a donation for the Orphanage. She agreed right away to Jane Ann's adoption. Percy and Agnes agreed as well, knowing that Jane Ann would still be in their family and visiting them as often as possible. They thought it all would turn out to be a very simple matter. Dudley, Dudley, and Fitch had the papers all drawn and the matter over and finished in no time! So it happened that Miss Jane Ann Perkins became the daughter of Mr. and Mrs. Harold Chance Rogers.

Jane Ann was the happiest one of them all. Especially so since the Jane Ann in the painting came to speak to her again on the evening before the adoption was final.

"Who are you really? What is your name?" Jane Ann had asked the misty figure who suddenly appeared beside her easel.

"I am Jane Ann Rogers, and I am now your Grandmother, Child." She had spoken softly.

Jane Ann knew her drawing of this beautiful lady had started the whole adoption thing. "Thank you for being my Grandmother," she replied softly. Then she was surprised to see all the others come forward one at a time. They all seemed to want to speak to her and give her a small message, as if it were a real birthday party!

"Look, Jane Ann, this is your Mother and her name is Dorothy." Grandmother Rogers said softly. A figure smelling of lavender came and gave a ghostly kiss to Jane Ann's cheek. Another figure appeared and Grandmother Rogers introduced her as Grandmother Perkins. She gave Jane Ann's hand a tender ghostly pat.

"All of us applaud what you have done so far and we will always be nearby for you." Grandmother Rogers said. Then they all disappeared leaving Jane Ann saying "Thank you!" to the air.

Harold and Emma loved being Jane Ann's parents. At first, they took their time moving all of Jane Ann's things to their house in the country outside London. As soon as everything was moved though, they had a celebration, a party "Just for the six of us!" Harold had teased, meaning for he, Emma, Jane Ann, the two dogs Oscar and O'Donnell, and the cat, Margie. This was Jane Ann's first experience with animals and she found them all to be great fun! The dogs took to her at once. The cat took longer, about a day and then Margie began following Jane Ann around everywhere. For cats to do that is unusual indeed.

Harold and Emma had a man and his wife, Petrie and Grace Hodgson who tended their household by doing the cleaning and cooking, and directing the gardeners who tended the grounds. Harold went once a week to his office at the Bank of London where he spent most all day. Emma sewed and crocheted and read to Jane Ann. She loved the old mythologies of Greece and Rome and especially the stories from India that her father had brought with him after being there for several years. Jane Ann loved all the stories. She thrived with all the love and attention she was getting.

Jane Ann's charcoal drawings and paintings became somewhat famous especially when Harold began to take them in to his office and then to hang them in the bank. It was not unusual for Jane Ann to draw or paint a scene of a large elephant standing in an elephant graveyard with a Hindu woman standing just in the forefront. No more unusual than her watercolor paintings of a peaceful English garden scene with a family seated on the grass watching a little child play. No matter what she created, it drew a great deal of interest.

One of the customers of the bank saw a painting of a toreador with a sad look on his face at the moment he pierced a huge bull in the heart. As it turned out, the painting was a perfect copy of one a famous artist had done over a century before in Madrid, Spain. The painting had never been circulated, but the customer had seen it on several occasions in a private family museum while visiting his sister who was living in Madrid with her husband. He told Harold about this. When Harold told Emma and Jane Ann, the ladies just smiled.

"I know it is a copy of one done before, Pa," Jane Ann had said. The artist who painted the original is Jose de Carlo and it was he who showed it to me."

"Showed it to you, how, Jane? How could that be?" Harold was genuinely puzzled about Jane Ann's gift to see spirit people, but it didn't bother him at all. The English people had always believed in the extraordinary and not just the obvious.

"I was trying to use oil paints for the first time last Spring, remember?" she reminded him.

He wasn't sure he did remember. After all, Emma was more involved in her materials than he was. He enjoyed the end result. "Not really, dear, but go ahead." He urged her.

"Well, Mr. de Carlo just appeared when I was having one of my headaches and told me how easy it was to use oils and not to worry too much about how to use them.

Harold didn't hear the rest of it. He was absolutely flabbergasted that she could ask a question or wonder about something and just get answers like that. He wondered if such a talent could be used to improve the world and make it a better place? Maybe no one HAD to be hungry, or sick, or . . . . maybe.

Emma interrupted his thoughts. "Harold, what in the world is going on about the painting? Jane Ann is so gifted, honestly, I believe she could draw or paint anything."

"Or see anyone or anything, too, perhaps?" He questioned. Then he decided he would have to stay quiet about this part of her gift. It was almost too preposterous to believe, even though he and Emma believed almost anything. Certainly they were open to accepting anything at all, especially after the first drawing they had seen of hers, the one of Mother Rogers, his own Mother, long gone into the spirit world!

Harold had gone to a number of people to find out what he could about extraordinary talents like Jane Ann's. He had spent some time reading and talking to scholars who knew something more (and he knew next to nothing) about this business of seeing or hearing the spirit people. Most anyone who knew anything shied away from talking to him openly at first, and it seemed to be a secret topic most folks were afraid of, but not Petrie.

It was a surprise to Harold. However, after weeks of investigation all over London and nearby villages, it was his own man, Petrie, in his own house, who could even speak with him about what was happening.

"The little girl took a bad hit on the head when she was just a wee one," Petrie had said in Harold's study. "What that does is open up a door somewhere in the mind, and that's when the spirit people can just walk in."

Harold did not feel too good about a "door being opened" in Jane Ann's mind, but he thoughtfully listened to Petrie. At least Petrie was trying to make rational sense of the extraordinary gift of Jane Ann's.

"The person just naturally sees and hears spirits most likely attracted to them by their own tendencies. In Jane Ann's case, she is a good and sweet person so she attracts good and sweet spirits to her." He rested his case.

"Hmmm." Harold said, "So who is going to guarantee that the only spirits she attracts to her will be good and sweet natured and so forth?" Harold wondered aloud. "I don't know about this. It seems to me that she would need to have some direction, some teacher who could show her how to keep out the others."

"Well, sir, she's got a gift here that she's been using a few years." Petrie answered carefully, knowing what little he did, that Jane Ann was injured at age three and began "seeing" not long afterwards when the headaches began, and now she was 14 years old. "It seems like pretty soon she will be moving more into being an adult female, and the way I figure it, either she will forget this part of her gift and quit seeing spirit people, or it will get more to where it takes over her mind all the time."

Harold suddenly realized this was entirely possible! She might just stop it or it might grow to overtake her whole thinking! Perhaps it was time he and Emma found new interests for her. Perhaps painting and drawing should be put aside for awhile and she should take up horseback riding, or be encouraged to have more friends over to play games like lawn croquet or cards or anything. He thanked Petrie, and then he went to find Emma.

Of course, Emma thought he was making a mountain out of a small hill. The likelihood of anything, any interest "taking over" Jane Ann's mind seemed ludicrous at best. "Besides," Emma told Harold, "Jane Ann already knows how to ride a horse, plus play lawn croquet, plus play cards! And there are no young people around here. Have you forgotten, my dear husband, we live in the country!" She laughed suddenly. "You are making too, too much of this. Jane Ann is perfectly normal, and gifted, and beautiful, and a kind and generous person. You have to stop fidgeting about this!" She dismissed it.

Harold finally did, too. After he began to think of the three of them having a change of scenery, going to live in another country perhaps. He thought of Italy or Greece. Perhaps they could go for a year or so just to give Jane Ann a look at people and art in another place far removed from England and its old spirits hanging around everywhere.

Then a customer came in to the bank all up in arms about going to the new country, America, and especially to the western part. It seems that there had been a gold rush in one of the western provinces and people were absolutely digging up riches in their own yard. He told such fantastic stories that Harold went home immediately and announced to Emma and Jane Ann that they were going to America!

Jane Ann had been looking forward to the Harper's School of Etiquette and Manners in London the following Autumn when new classes started. Emma had already written and Jane Ann had been admitted provisionally on her knowledge of literature and art and mathematics. She was invited for a visit in two weeks. At that time she would be interviewed and given final approval to become a live-in student the coming year. If they were going to America though, the visit to Harper's would have to be put off.

"Yes, of course, you can always come back for Harper's, Jane Ann, but we may never get this good an opportunity for an adventure in America again!" Harold was tickled about the idea of the three of them digging up gold and having a grand time in a western province in a whole new country! "In fact, Jane Ann, if you will agree that we should all go together on this adventure, I promise you that you can come back the summer of next year, also that you can stay at Percy's and Agnes's house, and that you can look over Harper's. Then if you want to attend that school, bang! It will all work out perfectly." He had convinced her! He was so excited and, as a matter of fact, so was Emma!

Emma had not realized it earlier, she had been so happy settled into real family life, but now she caught Harold's enthusiasm. She knew she had enough peace and quiet the past few years to last awhile. Something in her longed for the adventures they used to go on, those sudden trips to the Alps, the boat ride down the Nile River in Egypt. Seeing the strange and mysterious was an allure she could not pass up. Emma's vote was "yes" let's go!"

Jane Ann watched both Harold and Emma through their decision making. Never in a million years would she have thought of going away to a strange country to dig for gold and to have adventures. She loved Mama and Papa though and, where they went, she would go! "Yes, yes," Jane Ann joined them in dancing around. "Yes, let's go!"

Harold began setting everything in motion immediately, and before too many days had passed, he had booked them on a ship to New York in America. They had a stateroom, not very large, but just the right size for family and friends to fill with goodies. Jane Ann made sure she had enough paper, charcoal, and paints to last her the trip. Percy and Agnes made sure to load it with all the delicacies they would have liked had they been going to a strange land (even while affirming to themselves they would never be so impulsive). Everyone wondered what they would find available once they got to America.

Jeremy came to the ship to tell them goodbye and to bring them up to date on his attending college very soon, something which Agnes's cousin had made sure was going to happen. At 20, Jeremy was a tall, handsome lad. He hugged them all goodbye then he promised to meet them in New York someday. He intended also to stand on the docks and watch their ship pull out from port this day.

As he hugged Jane Ann, he kissed her on the cheek and whispered, "You must be careful whom you give your heart to in America, Janie." Then he had held her a little away so he could look at her a long time as if to etch a memory of her forever in his mind. "I say, Janie, are you still seeing spirit people? If so, dear girl, perhaps they can help take care of you and Harold and Emma."

Jane Ann had not wanted to let go of Jeremy. Though they had missed a few of their growing up years together, still she felt as close to him as if he were her brother, and she wished he would go with them. She wished she had thought of asking early enough to convince Harold and Emma to allow Jeremy to go with them! But she had not. So she let him go and then she leaned against the ship's rails watching him wave goodbye from the docks.

CHAPTER 6

The beginning of their trip by ship was uneventful and a little boring for Jane Ann. She made friends soon though with twins from a country village far outside London. The twins' names were George and Georgette and they were two years older than she. Georgette and Jane Ann were interested in much the same things. They talked about Harper's. Both of the girls planned to go back to London the following summer. They made a pact to keep in touch and to schedule their return to London and to Harper's at the same time.

Seventeen-year-old George, though, was interested in Jane Ann. Three weeks into the trip, George confessed to Jane Ann that he had a mad crush on her and wanted to propose that they give each other a kiss and something to remember each other by. They felt this would make their trip a thing to remember. Jane Ann and Georgette giggled; however, Jane Ann had agreed, and she gave George a drawing she had made one evening of he and Georgette. Jane Ann also allowed George to kiss her on the cheek. Their bargain was sealed. All three young people would remember the occasion for a long time.

Each of them vowed to keep in touch with each other and, if that happened to be impossible, they also each promised to keep a daily journal of what was happening in their lives. Surely they would be able to get together at least once more before they got too old and share the adventures they had recorded in their journals. George laughed and said that would surely "be a hoot!" The girls agreed. He intended also to look for Jane Ann some day because of their swapping gifts and that kiss on the cheek.

George and Georgette were impatient to see their Uncle and his family whom they did not know. Their Uncle Bob had traveled from Boston to be in New York when their ship docked. Both of them hung over the railing looking for Uncle Bob. Finally George spotted him. He gave a yell and then turned around and waved to Jane Ann and pointed to the fellow waving from the docks. Jane Ann could only wish it was Jeremy there waiting for her and Emma and Harold. However, she was glad for George and Georgette.

As Harold, Emma, and Jane Ann disembarked, their luggage was already being loaded on a carriage. As they made their way through the unkempt streets of New York City, all of them felt a pang of loneliness for London. "Oh, well," Jane was thinking, "Papa says we can go back when we want to." Looking out the carriage at the trash strewn street, Jane Ann secretly WANTED to go back to London then and that moment!

They found a nice hotel, one that had been recommended to them, and then a small café where they were able to get a decent supper. It was not British cooking, but it was palpable. Jane Ann wondered what Boston would be like for George and Georgette, and she hoped they would be happy there. Already she was missing them!

The next morning Harold checked with the desk to see if a message and tickets had arrived for their trip west to California. They had not. The attendant apologized. The following morning, the attendant apologized again. For a week, they heard the same apology. That was about as long as either of the women wanted to linger in New York, so Harold began to look for ways to get them on their way West.

He finally settled upon a train which would take them as far as St. Louis. From St. Louis, Harold assured the ladies that they would be able to obtain a wagon and all that they needed, including a guide, to lead them straight overland to California. He sent several telegrams ahead to St. Louis to make sure they would not be disappointed or suffer the same kind of delay they had in New York. Of course, the trip on across to California would take at least three more months, but it would be such an "exciting adventure!" At least, that is what Harold tried to convince Emma and Jane Ann.

Emma had not lost her enthusiasm for a good adventure. She did rather long for Petrie and Grace to be there looking out for them though. Instead, she pulled herself up and dug out two books from their luggage. One was her favorite about Greek mythology, and the other a thin dime store novel about the American west. If she could interest Jane Ann into taking turns reading and even acting out the stories, then it might be an interesting adventure for Jane Ann, too! Surely the trip would feel faster and shorter if they were occupied in some way.

They arrived in St. Louis in 1852 to find unexpected surprises for them. They had never seen people walking around the streets with loaded guns before. Harold made a mental note to write an article for the London Daily Express about visiting St. Louis. It would make the Londoners even more glad to stay home, or else it would spur adventurers like themselves (Harold and Emma) to immediately pack their bags for America. Also, in 1849, St Louis suffered a year of disaster. Fifteen city blocks were devastated by a great fire including 23 steamboats along the riverfront. During the same year, an epidemic of cholera took thousands of lives. City officials were still trying to decide whether to drain Chouteau's Pond and sell the land to the Pacific Railroad.

Harold kept a close eye on both Emma and Jane Ann. He joked to them that in the event things got a little sticky, they could all run away together! That made a really funny visual picture (them running away) Harold thought. But when he tried to explain its humor to the ladies, both Emma and Jane Ann failed to get the humor.

Then when Harold began to think about any of them shooting a firearm, he knew he, for one, had never fired one. Of course, Emma and Jane Ann had not either. How could he know whether they could at all? Certainly, it would be a hard thing to point a firearm at another human being. Surely the ladies never could. Finally, Harold decided they would never need to, and he shook his doubts off and began to make a list of items they would need on their trek westward.

Later, when he took his list into the general store, the man behind the counter was so helpful as to tell him uproariously funny stories about other travelers gone on before them who had not known, as the gentleman phrased it, "their fanny from a hole in the ground" when it came to choosing what to fill a wagon with. Somehow that description did not sit well with Harold. He felt it might describe himself too well at the moment. Since the man seemed to know just what one would need for traveling west, Harold decided to let him have a free hand filling their wagon. It was a great mystery why none of the instructions in his telegrams had been followed already by the travel agency in St. Louis. Harold had been very specific about choosing an experienced guide to get the wagon and provisions ready so no time would be spent in St. Louis just WAITING to prepare for their journey. Of course, the agency's clerk had no explanation. Great mysteries were already abounding in this new country!

Some of the items chosen by the store clerk seemed a bit preposterous later as Harold and Emma were going through and checking their list with what they actually came away with for their journey. The man had added in three firearms, one of them being a rifle, and the other two being handguns. Harold knew nothing about either, however, the clerk assured the ladies that they could learn whatever they needed to learn as they were traveling on west. The clerk had also added that he "really doubt that any of you will be called upon to shoot a firearm." Harold had thought that another box of canned goods would have been preferred over two guns.

When the guide finally appeared to help them load the wagon, he was about as big a braggart as either Harold, Emma or Jane Ann had ever heard. The man kept telling the same stories over and over again about "shooting bloodthirsty injuns" and how they were a bad lot and to be feared. That was not at all the idea Harold had of the American Indian. He and Emma had rather another image of a wise man or woman able to commune with nature and the nature spirits.

"I rather think Jane Ann will like the American Indian." Harold chuckled to Emma. "Can't you see her teaching a young Indian girl English with our British accent?"

"And," Emma joined in, "The Indian girl teaching Jane Ann a native dialect or whatever tribal language she speaks?" Actually it all sounded like a fine idea.

Jane Ann just arched her eyebrows in mock surprise at their discussion of what could happen. She knew she loved them dearly no matter what.

The guide then assured Harold and Emma that they had ample supplies for their trip to California and, if they ran out of anything, all they had to do was stop at a trading post or at a military post and there would be goods available for them. He also told them to be on the lookout for small towns because, as fast as people were heading west, there should be new towns sprouting up all the way across to California.

Finally, they were outfitted, and their covered wagon was ready. Harold had taken sufficient lessons (so the guide had assured him) so he could drive the wagon safely to San Francisco. They had gone over their maps and directions not once but several times. Even Jane Ann had to "find" their directions on the guide's map not once but three times to prove she would not get lost either if they became separated. Then they were directed out of St. Louis toward California. At least, they THOUGHT their guide had seen them off toward the west. For awhile they also BELIEVED they were going in the right direction. They followed the route the guide had shown them over and over just as closely as they could for almost three weeks.

Each night they would stop and build a fire and camp out, eat and then sleep, only to rise before daylight to start all over again. Nowhere was there a road or a level path to ride on. Either they were tilted one way or the other. Either they were going through clumps of trees like forests, or over hills, or around areas that seemed impassable. Eventually, Harold tired of the routine. There was certainly no adventure to be had doing the same things over and over. The guide should have gone with them part way, perhaps even all the way. Harold would have preferred that. He wondered why he had not thought of that! He was also now thinking that he should have hired a skilled horseman to drive the wagon for them. Yet, he knew he must continue to make a game of it, and to pretend to know what he was doing so the girls would not become frightened or lose hope of seeing their destination. After all, other families had made it across, and many others had gone the whole way and were writing stories for the newspapers. Some were even writing about their grand adventures in dime novels or pocketbooks. Harold and Emma had read some of them. Jane Ann had read some also. They had cheered at the courage and fortitude of the people.

Eventually, Harold attempted to get the two ladies interested in learning to shoot. After all, they had two pistols and one rifle, and it would be a waste not to learn something about shooting. Where else would it be safer? After endless attempts to convince Emma and Jane, finally Emma gave in and told Harold they would practice. So, Harold stopped the wagon and got down and, bowing to each one, he helped the ladies climb down and begin their "practice shooting."

Unfortunately the guide had not obtained any bullets for either the rifle or the pistols. Bullets had not been on Harold's list.

Emma was not pleased and she let Harold know in no uncertain terms. "What a dreadful person not to even remember that we may have to hunt for our food!" Emma had exclaimed. Thereafter, she refused to look at or even touch a gun. She would not allow Jane Ann to so much as look at them either. Harold himself began to wonder that should they need to hunt whether he could use a knife sufficiently well to kill, skin and prepare the game for dinner. Finally, he put the guns away.

During one stop, a small band of Indians who called themselves Kickapoo came into camp and asked for meat. They spoke a few words of English enough to make clear what they wanted. "We from East of here," one of them had said while pointing in that direction.

Harold did not feel good about refusing them, but actually meat was one of the things that had to be hunted and killed fresh every day. Unless you were lucky enough to have an advisor like Harold found who told him to take along a small cage of chickens. Thus far, Harold, Emma and Jane Ann had eaten chicken at least twice a week during their journey. These chickens were a secret he did not choose to share with the Kickapoo. He was glad to share their vegetable stew, however, even though he knew they would not have vegetables for long either. Already the pots of plants were using up far too much of their precious water.

Harold thought the group of lads, one old gentleman and four young ones, the However, later that evening, while they were asleep, the Kickapoo came back and stole the cage of chickens and broke several of their pots holding growing vegetables. They also stole the three saddles that were securely stored underneath the blankets. The blankets were also missing.

The way Harold knew their thieves were the same people they had shared their dinner with was when the men started yodeling and yelling at the top of their lungs after they were loaded up and ready to leave. Harold, Emma and Jane Ann woke up right away and looked out from under the wagon where they were sleeping.

"That settles it," Emma said sternly. "We are all going to sleep inside the wagon from now on every night of the way!"

"Well, at least they didn't kill us," Jane Ann said trying to be funny. However, neither Harold nor Emma laughed.

After that, Harold tried in earnest to learn how to shoot first the rifle, then one of the pistols by practicing sighting. Soon, when they came across a trading post, ammunition would be one of the first things they would get from the shopkeeper. After only a few hours of sighting and several days practice, Harold felt he had done his best. It would be far better to check their maps from there on and see if they were getting close to a trading post or perhaps even a town.

"Oh, well," Harold sighed, "We will just have to stop at a trading post or even more appealing, a real town. We can rest awhile before we head out again." The trip was beginning to be more trouble than adventure. But maybe not, Harold hoped, as he continued to mentally reason with himself. Maybe the first part of the trip, being so close to St. Louis and "civilization" was almost barren because one could easily turn back and try again at a later time. Harold, though, chose to forge ahead, to look for a trading post, a town, a little group of people whom (their "Guide" in St. Louis had promised them) lived along the way.

Jane Ann was hoping they had more than that to look forward to out west in California.

"We are going to have an absolutely delightful adventure! Look up, ladies!" Harold intended to say every half hour.

Harold kept the mules walking in the day time and resting at night. He noticed the grass did not grow as high or thick in the direction they were heading. He hoped eventually it would be better though, and so he kept going forward. What he did not know is that instead of going forward toward California, that he had been started off (by the Guide back in St. Louis) heading in a northern direction toward the Black Hills and a dangerous mountain pass.

As the three settled down hoping for an early sleep that night, Jane Ann appeared restless. When Emma asked what was wrong, she complained of a "terrible headache." Within a few minutes, Jane Ann asked to be excused to sit outside in the air. Emma and Harold both went to sit with her.

The embers in their campfire were burning low when Harold murmured, "That should be enough to keep the critters away." He sat down beside the ladies.

"Mama," Jane Ann said, and then she stopped as if in mid-thought.

"Yes," Emma said, "Go on, dear." Emma wondered what was troubling Jane Ann.

"Mama," Jane Ann began again, "Remember the spirit people I see sometimes who talk to me?"

Emma nodded and said, "Yes," and certainly Harold remembered also.

"They are telling me that we should stay away from snow, that we are not to go into any mountains or try to go through any mountain pass, that it will be extremely dangerous. In fact, it would be so dangerous that our lives would be in jeopardy." She did not know how to put it any other way. They had shown her the same images over and over for several days by that time. What they were showing her was a covered wagon traveling through and over a mountain pass being caught and buried in an avalanche. Jane Ann had trembled as she was telling them about the danger.

Harold began to assure her, "Well, you are not to worry your head one whit over that, dear Jane Ann, for we are definitely not going over or through any mountains." He had not been told of any mountains until they went across the Rocky Mountains, and then again as they got near to California. He did not think that in almost four weeks they could be anywhere near that. Besides, they did not pass any military post or trading post from the list of several that they would go near. Harold really thought they were going in the right direction.

Emma hugged Jane Ann. If it were not for their ridiculous ideas about adventure and fun, Jane Ann would probably be visiting Harper's School for Etiquette and Manners in London about then. "Let's just say our prayers, Jane Ann, and believe that we are not going through or over any mountains. We will stop at the first settlement and hire somebody to lead us the entire rest of the way. I promise you we will!" And Emma glared at Harold over Jane Ann's shoulder.

Harold nodded in agreement. It sounded like a good idea to him, too.

Harold then asked Jane Ann if it was his mum, Mother Rogers, showing Jane Ann the avalanche, however, she said it was not. "Who, then, my dear is giving you such a fright?"

"It's a beautiful Indian woman, Papa. She is dressed in a white buckskin dress with fringe all over the sleeves and at the edge of the skirt. Her hair is white, and she has the kindest look on her face." Jane Ann described her.

They finally all dropped off to sleep in the wagon as soon as Jane Ann settled down after telling them about what the spirit people showed her. It was almost daylight when a horrible stench awoke them one by one. Emma smelled it first. Then Harold. Finally so did Jane Ann.

"Good heavens," Harold complained, "It smells like rotten fish or dead worms or something absolutely disgusting!" He got up and started looking around.

Emma and Jane Ann crept about in the wagon looking through first one box then another, and into all the corners wondering all the time what in the world could smell like that. Finally, with the first light of day, they discovered that a skunk had taken shelter just beneath the left front wheel of their wagon. Not only had the skunk taken shelter but it probably had marked with its horrible odor everything remotely in its path.

"It will be days or perhaps even longer before the smell wears off." Harold groaned.

"Wash it off!" Emma told Harold. "We cannot ride with that smell following us everywhere. We will get deathly ill."

"But, dear, the water is low. We must find a creek or river, and maybe then we can just drive the front of the wagon in and clean it. We certainly dare not use our drinking water."

Both Emma and Jane Ann knew Harold was right. It was a long time to California. The guide had warned them about deserts. They would just have to accept the odor for what it was and do the best they could. Actually, once they got going again in daylight, the smell grew less offensive. Or perhaps they became accustomed to it. Either way, they kept going but were now actively watching and looking for people and little villages, even for Indian tents or tipis as the guide had called them.

Harold joked about it saying, "Soon, very soon" that they would see someone and when they did, they would just sop and ask them if it was possible to find another shorter route to California. Or maybe they could even go by ship. One man in St. Louis had told Harold about a southern route which would take them down the Mississippi River in a steamboat, then they could transfer in New Orleans to a ship, and then they would sail around the Americas to dock in California. Actually, as the man had described it, they would dock in San Francisco, exactly where they wanted to be!

"Oh, Harold!" Emma had exclaimed.

"Papa, how could you choose this awful wagon over such a fun sounding ride aboard a ship?" Jane Ann had been surprised that Harold had not chosen that more scenic route. What a pleasure it might have been aboard a riverboat and a ship! Oh, well. "Papa, let's do it as soon as we find someone who can point us in the right direction!" Jane Ann had pleaded.

"Oh, yes, indeed yes. Let's!" Emma had added. She suddenly couldn't wait to find someplace civilized or even just find some people again. Somebody surely could tell them how to get to the Mississippi, and maybe even help them get to wherever a river-boat could be found. How wonderful that would be.

When they camped that night and then woke the next morning, snow was blanketing the ground around and in front of them. For a time, Harold thought he could see absolutely nothing but white all around and over them. Then gradually, he began to spot large trees reaching up from beneath the snow. Somewhere straight ahead there would have to be a clear road or pathway well-traveled, Harold reasoned to himself. We are going to keep going! That was the only way he could figure out how NOT to panic the ladies, and how to finally get someplace where they could get help.

Hour after hour the horses pulled the wagon through the snow. In order to help them, Harold would stop and let them rest awhile, then he'd spur them on. When they stopped, he threw out the heavier objects from the wagon. Neither lady objected, and even if they had, he knew it would be the only way they could keep on going. Pulling a wagon in the rising snow would eventually cause the horses to drop dead of exhaustion.

Finally, Harold saw what he thought might be a clearing at last! It seemed a little lower than the snowy areas he had already traveled, and so in desperation, with hope growing in his heart, Harold moved into what he thought was a safe area. As soon as they got going good in the supposed clearing, a giant tree cracked and made a loud avalanche of snow fell from high above, and their wagon went plummeting down. Even while it was happening, all three of them thought of the image Jane Ann had seen in the warning by the spirits about the snow. Then, in a moment, they were buried below it. Even hours later, if anyone had been watching them, they would have seen snow continuing to avalanche down the mountains and piling onto the already buried wagon.

CHAPTER 7

Jane Ann thought she was dreaming . . . . or that she was already dead.
Her own Mother, Dorothy, the Lady in lavender was calling her name.
She was calling Jane Ann to "WAKE UP." Grandmother Rogers was also
calling her to wake up. Many spirit people were calling her name and telling
her to wake up. However, Jane Ann had no feeling in her body. She had no
feeling at all. She wondered if that had happened to bless her because the
air was so cold. Surely, if she were dead, she would answer the spirit people
by moving outside her physical body and becoming like them. Yet, if she
was still alive, why was it she could not feel anything, and therefore, she
could not release herself from whatever was holding her still.

"Mama! Papa," she started trying to say but could not. Mama! Papa!"
Where are you?" She could only THINK of calling them. Maybe they were
all three frozen, trapped beneath the snow. She tried to speak aloud again,
but she knew it was still speaking inside her head. "I tried," she spoke with
her thoughts to the Spirit people. "I tried to tell them what you showed
me. I am sorry I could not make it clear enough." All she could hear was
a soothing shush that lulled her back to unconsciousness.

The wind in the trees woke her next. She was still trapped and unable
to move. She wondered if she were paralyzed and that is why she had no
feeling in her body. But, how could she continue to live in her head without
feeling anything? She was determined not to fall into unconsciousness
again. Jane Ann began to recite everything she had read since the age of
five. Stories that she had long ago forgotten came into mind and she recited
each one of them in her head. On about the fifth or sixth story, she began
to feel a sudden cold chill shaking her body. She could feel! Or could she?

It was confusing. She could have sworn she had felt a chill, or at least some very cold air. Perhaps she was buried under mounds of snow, deep within the earth, and every once in awhile the wind would blow and chill air would reach her. Perhaps. Then she heard the wind again, a soft moaning as it blew through the leaves in the trees. It was blowing snow across the way through the air and off the leaves on the trees. It was blowing with a whistling and a sad moaning. Jane Ann listened intently. She continued reciting stories over and over inside her head.

Then she heard a shout from way off. It was a voice calling! It seemed far way, many miles away. Then another call was heard. And another. Someone was coming! "At last (Jane thought) "we are going to be saved!" She was thinking of the long way across desolate land week after week, and then of being buried under the snow, and then finally found! It was no longer inside her head. It was real. All those days without seeing anyone but a scruffy band of vagabonds, and now to be saved by friendly persons, but she wondered who they were. She could feel her heart beating faster and faster. That was good. Keep beating! Keep beating! Then there was silence. No sounds. Stillness again. She could feel her heart beating again. All was quiet. A moment later, she heard the voices again. It was closer this time, coming closer. She almost believed she heard the sound of feet crunching ice and snow. She felt hot liquid in her eyes running down her temples into her hair. Tears! It must be salty tears, warm from within her eyes! "Oh, dear God, if I am alive, then let Mama and Papa be alive, too. Thank You! Thank You!" She promised to herself never to be ashamed of crying again. She would cry freely in public and never think a thing about it again. Salty tears melt the snow. Melt the snow. Melt the snow.

"Hi ye! Hi yo!" A voice called sounding close to her head, and then continuing to speak words she did not understand. Hands were digging at the snow around her. More than one voice was speaking now, calling as if to each other, as if urging each other on. Or maybe they were calling to her and Mama and Papa to "hold on," but she could not be sure what language they were speaking. She just knew for sure they were digging them out of the snow. Soon . . . . soon . . . .

Like a vision in a dream, the woman in the white fringed dress appeared before Jane Ann's eyes and smiled. She was standing with her arms outstretched. Just seeing her made Jane Ann feel safer. "Stay with me," she was thinking, "please don't leave me."

At the same time, several different voices grunted and yelled very loud. Suddenly she was exposed to the light of the sun and it blinded her eyes. She could see nothing but a panorama of white light shot full of colored stars. Yet she was beginning to hear the voices better. Gentle but strong hands lifted her. A voice yelled something again but she could not understand what. Then as she was lifted up, unconsciousness mercifully drew her back into the darkness. The last thing she heard was the gentle voice of Woman in White saying, "Now . . . . "

The next time she awoke, she was on an animal skin travois that somehow was attached to a horse dragging her through the snow. "Hello," she began in a voice that shook with weakness, "Who are you?"

The persons with her, the one leading the horse, no one around her could hear her. She could hear them talking. She wanted someone to hear her, someone had to hear her. She continued to try to speak. She even tried to speak louder, maybe even to yell. Then the horse stopped. Faces came down close to hers.

She was looking into the eyes of three young Sioux Indians, she guessed ages between fourteen and seventeen. A voice behind her sounded deeper and she guessed that one was older. Whatever it was that he said prompted one of the younger ones to reach into a bag attached to a rope which was hanging around his shoulders, and he withdrew a blanket. Then she felt a soft, warm blanket smelling of sunshine being draped across her. It fell across her head, then hands quickly pulled it down and tucked it under her chin. The eyes of the young man placing the blanket seemed very kind. Although she did not understand what he was saying, it made her feel better. That time she allowed herself to go into unconsciousness again. If she were being treated so kindly, then so were Mama and Papa.

The young hunters had left their encampment near the Grande River before daybreak with the intention of finding and bringing back to the camp more game than anyone had seen all week. Many hunting parties had gone out and brought back small game. Most of their own fathers had been hunting and they had returned with a deer or a few squirrels. The young hunters then decided it was their turn!

Red Cloud was the eldest at 29. He was the nephew of the Chief of their peoples, Sitting Bull. Red Cloud was a quiet young man who kept to himself more than the others. He was a hero at age 14 when he sneaked into a Crow village and was chased by the Crow. Instead of being afraid, he took the coup stick his father had given him and he touched one of the Crow warriors with it. His own Sioux warriors were riding in at that moment hoping to save him from harm, and they saw the coup made by the young brave. Not a hair on the Crow warrior's head had been harmed. Instead, Red Cloud had counted coup, a feat that was very rare even for a seasoned warrior. Before that time he had been called "Slow" by his Father because of his deliberate and thoughtful way of doing things. That day that he made coup on the Crow warrior changed how others saw him, and his Father gave him his new name, "Red Cloud," which he had been given by a White Buffalo Cow in a vision.

On this particular morning, Red Cloud had watched the others and he decided he would ride out of camp to hunt with them. One of the others, Rain, had bid him welcome, and Red Cloud had known it was a sincere welcome. They had accepted him gladly.

Rain was the youngest member of the little band. He was 16 years old and well favored by many of the elders and warriors in their camp. Twice he had ridden hard to warn the men when they were out hunting and the camp was threatened. Another time, he had saved the life of a girl only two seasons old who had fallen into a stream when he jumped into the waters and brought her to safety. Rain seemed destined to act, to make instant decisions, to overcome big odds. Red Cloud called him "Brave Heart" and the name would have stuck but for the fact that his own Mother had named him "Rain" because of the raging storm that was going on when he was born.

Red Cloud had teased his friend, "A mother's son is a good man. Mark my words, Rain, you are still a Brave Heart!" The whole camp had cheered and whistled and agreed with Red Cloud. Rain was easily liked by everyone. He had a funny sense of humor but also great dignity. When the occasion needed laughter, Rain could think of something to say or do that was funny. When the occasion needed levity, he could lower his head and pray sincerely from his heart.

The other two young men were 15 year old twins, Left Hand and Right Hand, both had been named by their Father because he had wanted them to grow up thinking they needed to always stand together. "That way, they will never be enemies, but always brothers!" he had told everyone at their birth. Both young men were grateful for an opportunity to show their skills.

Left Hand and Right Hand were pulling both their horses tied securely to a travois that was carrying a large buffalo cow. Red Cloud was leading the horse pulling the travois that was carrying the white girl. Rain was alternately helping Red Cloud keep the horse straight on the hidden path, or running ahead to see the landmarks and make sure they were going in the right direction. It was easy to get lost, especially in the Black Hills. The area was hard to identify landmarks in, and some persons had been known to go into the hills and never return. Each of the hunters had been wondering how the white girl came to be where she was in the Black Hills.

Rain whistled so the others would know to follow the sound of his voice. He could not help wondering what an immense help it would be to all the people in camp when they came in with the big buffalo cow. Everyone would eat well for awhile! None of the children would be hungry for a long time. Also, the whole cow, hide, bones and all would surely serve them all well during the winter. Rain felt very satisfied. He was very thankful to the Great Spirit who had blessed them, who had caused this small hunting party to make just a few more steps into the wild hills where spirits roam freely to find not only a White Buffalo but also a white girl as well! What a day!

Red Cloud was thinking almost the same thing, wondering more about the girl and where she had come from, and if there were others with her, who were they and where were they now?

At first, their hunters had seen only the White Buffalo, and they had been unable to believe their eyes. Surely it was the biggest buffalo any of them had ever seen! Then when they loosened it from the snow and lifted it up onto the travois, there underneath lay the body of the white girl. It was amazing that she was alive at all!

Red Cloud wondered how long it had taken the cow to die? How long had the girl been laying under the cow? How had this girl crawled under the cow anyway with broken bones and cuts like she had? Or had the cow lain down on the girl to save her? He thought for a moment how they would feel if the girl died on the travois and was never to know that she had been saved? But that could not happen. He had seen her eyes open once. They were blue like the morning sky, and her matted and frozen hair was red like the sun.

Finally, the hunters came slowly into camp pulling their catch amid the yodels and shouts that welcomed them. Everyone was clapping their hands and dancing around in celebration. Of course they did! No longer was it an everyday thing for the experienced hunters to come in with a buffalo. The buffalo had started "hiding from the white man," so their Chief Sitting Bull had told them. Now here were four young hunters who had put all the warriors and elders to shame with the biggest buffalo any of them had ever seen! Not only was it big, it was a White Buffalo as well, and that meant someone must have had a vision or a message from White Buffalo Woman not long before!

Rain, along with Red Cloud, was scanning the crowd now. Everyone seemed to be talking at once, and some of the mothers and sisters were wanting to pat the hunters on their backs to let them know how brave they were and what good hunters they are. The young girls of marrying age were being as forward as the men and old women, and even worse as the little children running over and touching as many of the animals, especially the buffalo, as they got close enough.

Red Cloud smiled and shook his head. Usually he would want to run and hide when the commotion started just like then, but not this time. This afternoon he felt honored as if bound by some secret code of duty or some feeling that he could not identify to remain with Rain, Left Hand, and Right Hand. They seemed to all be staying together, putting up with compliments, with praise long overdue for some of them perhaps, waiting for they were not sure exactly what. Nevertheless, looking, watching closely, almost desperately for Grandfather, or for Rena, and either would do. There was no one else they could turn the red haired girl over to, no one.

Finally Rain spotted Grandfather. "Hi ho," Grandfather greeted Rain and the other hunters. "You have done very well indeed." Grandfather smiled a toothless grin. He was a very old man, no one knew exactly how old. Everybody called him "Grandfather" because he was the oldest man in the camp, maybe the oldest in the Sioux Nation! Even the great Chief of the whole Sioux peoples called him Grandfather. At least that is what Rain and the other hunters had been told in stories they had been hearing since they were very small children.

Grandfather's hair was white. It had been white as long as any of them could remember. His face was as wrinkled as dry parchment left in the wind and sun many years. Yet his body was tall and strong and, if you did not look at his wrinkled countenance, you might think he was much younger. He was, however, the wisest and kindest person many had ever known.

Grandfather greeted each of them by name. He whispered something special for each one of them. Whatever he whispered had great meaning for each young man. Then each bowed his head reverently and nodded. Grandfather patted each one's shoulder after speaking to them. Finally, he turned to the red-haired girl lying unconscious amid the noise and yelling and excitement in the camp.

He had never known a white girl or seen one this close before. He had seen a white man, yes. Chief Sitting Bull had insisted that they begin to get to know them. Grandfather wondered if Sitting Bull knew something from the spirits about the white people that the rest of them did not know yet. People talked about the way Sitting Bull wanted so bad to know the white man. No one understood it, Grandfather figured, no one except Chief Sitting Bull himself.

"No native peoples before Sitting Bull ever wanted anything to do with the white eyes." That's what Grandfather had told anyone who asked him. He had even warned Sitting Bull that he was courting an unknown future, but Sitting Bull had told him it was destiny. "They are our future, Grandfather," was all Chief Sitting Bull would say about it.

"Well, maybe destiny has come calling to us early," Grandfather whispered. Yet as he looked at this girl, so wan and pale, breathing ever so lightly, his heart went out immediately to her. He lifted the blanket gently. "Ah, she is hurt very bad." He said. There was blood matted on the travois where her right leg was. He could see the bones broken through the skin and torn muscles.

Grandfather motioned for Rain and Red Cloud to move the travois, and for Left Hand and Right Hand to scatter the crowd aside. Young girls were still clinging to Right Hand, and he had an embarrassed look on his face as if one of the girls had whispered one compliment too many. Then Red Cloud reached over and pushed him, and the girls let go so that Right Hand could do what Grandfather wanted.

Somehow they made it safely with the girl across the camp to Grandfather's tipi. He opened the flap and motioned them to bring the girl in very carefully "because her wounds are very serious." He cautioned them to be careful as they tenderly lifted her and deposited her gently onto the soft sleeping pallet.

The girl's breathing was beginning to wheeze now. Or maybe it had been wheezing down the mountainside and none of them had noticed because of the wind. Actually her sounds had been so weak, they could not hear her in the wind anyway.

Rain and Red Cloud looked at each other. Both young men said almost at the same time that they would wait outside to be called. Grandfather shook his head 'no.'

"There's no need to do that. Go and find Rena to help me with the girl. She was with the sick children earlier before I heard you coming back into camp. See if she's still there, or maybe out in the crowd. I need her to help me." He continued to move bowls and herbs around to find just the right one while he was talking. "You both, and all of you hunters, need rest and sleep. You have done your duty very well. Go get some praise, hear some good words. You can come back in the morning if you wish to be of help. Rena will stay with us tonight. Go! Go on!" He waved them away with his hands.

Then he reached down and pulled back the blanket to get a better look at the girl's feet and legs. "Ah!" he groaned. "There is where the blood is coming from." One foot was crushed. It appeared at first to be turned at an opposite angle to what it should be. This one would require a lot of work. Bones and bone chips stuck out in all directions. Blood was seeping from the wounds there and also from the long cut across the calf muscle of the same leg.

Rain and Red Cloud turned immediately and left to go get Rena.

Some of the older people in their camp said Rena was Grandfather's daughter, and some said his granddaughter. Whatever she was, she certainly knew medicine and healing as good as Grandfather. She had only married once long ago, someone said, when she was a young girl of sixteen. The man had been killed by a bear. Ever since then, Rena hated bears. She hated to hear anyone talking about bears. She had been known to pick up an iron skillet and throw it from the fire when she heard anyone bragging about their sacred animal being a bear. It might just be a woman's story, but all the children remembered it and they did not talk about bears around Rena.

Rain and Red Cloud had no trouble finding Rena. She had already heard that Grandfather had taken the white woman into their tent, and so she was already heading that way. Very quickly, both Rain and Red Cloud began to tell her what she would find when she got to Grandfather's tent.

"Ah ho," she nodded, "I thank you." She added, "You are very good hunters." She was not one to give praise lightly. What she said meant a lot to the two young men. "Just think how hard you will have to hunt to do better than you have this day!" Her eyes twinkled and she smiled, "Go on with you! Enjoy your fine day."

CHAPTER 8

The white girl moaned as Grandfather and Rena tended to her wounds. The upper part of her body must have been protected, and one of her legs, but the other leg and ankle were deeply cut and broken, oh, so many times that it took hours to put the pieces together. Rena had given her sips of the sleeping herb. Nothing is as painful as a broken bone. There was hardly any medicine that could ease that pain.

"Is it true, Grandfather," Rena asked, "that pain is not felt in the physical body but in the energy body which we cannot see?"

"Yes," Grandfather replied, "the invisible spirit body we carry around with us is where we feel pain."

"If this girl is asleep, or her mind is not conscious of what is happening, does she still know how much pain she is experiencing?" Rena continued her questions.

"If I cut the tail off a snake once. And then I cut the separated part again, will the snake experience the pain of the second cut?" Grandfather asked Rena.

She was puzzled. "Yes, I think so," she replied, "Perhaps because the spirit tail is still whole with the snake, with that part that feels?"

"Perhaps so," Grandfather said. "It would be hard to tell which one is illusion, the spirit tail or the real tail."

"Then," Rena continued, "Do we feel pain when we are asleep or unconscious as this girl is now?" Rena was watching Jane Ann moan and turn her head back and forth.

Grandfather touched Rena's arm lightly. "She will not remember most of it when she wakes, Rena." He assured her. The old man and the woman worked well together. Grandfather tended to setting the bones and suturing the long cut. Rena handed him the tools, cleaned the wounds, helped tie the knots in the sinew which he used for suturing. Occasionally, Rena wiped the girl's forehead with a wet cloth. Often she held her hand. Before they had finished, Rena was talking softly to her, telling her she would be fine, that this would one day be only a dream.

Together, Grandfather and Rena had tended worse wounds together before in others. Yet this girl seemed to touch a deep chord of sympathy in Rena. Perhaps she was thinking that she could have been her own daughter.

After hours of suturing and setting of bone chips, they had finished doing what they could for her. Rena helped Grandfather wrap and bind the bandages so they would stay on, as well as the wooden sticks wrapped in animal skin around the girl's ankle. If the ankle was disturbed before it began to knit back then she would perhaps be unable to walk. Even if the ankle was not disturbed, she would probably have a pronounced limp.

Off and on during the night, the girl moaned. Sometimes her breath would begin wheezing again. Grandfather was concerned about fluid in her chest. He lit the sage and sweetgrass again and shook it all around the outside edge of the sleeping pallet. He prayed again and again throughout the night for the Great Spirit to heal the girl, and to bless the young warriors who had found her. Toward the morning, the girl seemed to relax and sleep sounder. Grandfather, too, had dozed off.

By then, Rena had already had a long nap and so she sat up and began her prayers. "Great Spirit, bless the warriors," she prayed, "and heal this girl for she has been sent to us by White Buffalo Woman as a sign and a blessing to our peoples." Silently she visualized an image of the Great Force of Healing traveling around the girl's sleeping mat. Then she, too, rested.

The next morning, Jane Ann woke in a strange place. She found herself on a comfortable mat in a tipi. It was not just an ordinary tent, but it seemed to be a magical one. Her eyes took in the whole place beginning with the hole in the top of the tipi where the poles crossed, where the light from the sun shown in. The heavy fabric stretched very wide making a larger circle the closer it came to the ground. It was securely fastened to the ground in many places and so appeared very permanent and secure. Inside the tipi, in the sunlight streaming in the smoke hole, Jane Ann could see personal things belonging to the two Indians who sat looking at her. They watched her patiently.

Rena reached to offer Jane Ann a cup of tea. In her native Sioux language, she spoke soothingly telling the girl she was safe and would be well and not to be afraid. Grandfather smiled at her.

Jane Ann looked first at the woman. Her hair was long and dark and fell easily across her shoulders down her back. She wore a long print dress decorated with the skins of animals, perhaps to make it warmer for the winter. Soft moccasins covered her feet and were tied around her legs (Jane Ann could not see but imagined them) above her knees.

Jane Ann leaned up on one arm and sipped the warm tea. It was delicious. She could hear the woman speaking but she did not understand the language.

"Tea," Jane Ann said clearly several times. Each time she would sip and swallow the tea she would repeat the word T E A. After about the third time, Rena smiled, and nodded, and then spoke the Sioux word for tea. After a few minutes, the two were naming everything within sight, Jane Ann in English and Rena in Sioux.

Grandfather was amazed at the demonstration of unity. Each one communicating and, at the same time, teaching one another a whole new language. He chuckled at the sight. It was certainly something to tell Red Cloud and Sitting Bull about at the next meeting. He laughed again, aloud this time. Both women stopped and looked at him.

The girl looked tired. "Rest, rest," he urged her knowing she did not understand.

Rena immediately showed her what the word meant by closing her hands together and leaning on them with her eyes closed. The girl seemed to understand immediately and repeated the word over and over. Then she told them what the word was in her language. "Rest." She said to them. She decided immediately to be still for a few moments and she watched them through half closed eyes.

Someone outside the entrance to the tipi cleared his throat.

Grandfather called, "Come in, Red Cloud, the girl is awake and better now."

Red Cloud came in without even wondering how Grandfather knew it was he. The old man was so wise he had many tricks to teach them all.

Red Cloud approached where the girl was on the mat and he leaned down. He still had one hand behind his back.

Jane Ann opened her eyes. She smelled lavender and wondered if the spirit of her Mother, Dorothy, was close by and going to communicate with her. But she did not have a headache, and usually a headache was the warning that the spirit people were close by.

Instead, the tall Indian who had come in and squatted down beside her mat was still watching her. Now she got a good look at him. His bronzed face had a long nose and gentle eyes with thin lips. He seemed to be waiting for her to say something.

"Ah, ho," Jane Ann said in greeting after having just learned that from Rena and Grandfather.

"Ah, ho," Red Cloud answered and then he grinned. He brought his hand from behind his back and presented her with a small bouquet of lavender flowers.

Jane Ann smiled and said, "Thank you very much," and then added, "Ah, ho" and the man laughed again. She wondered where in the frozen land he could find beautiful lavender flowers. But Rena, however, knew they were from some mother's pot of herbs.

"She has good teeth, Grandfather," Red Cloud said for lack of conversation. He wished very much that he could speak with the girl.

"Good teeth for a girl or a horse?" Grandfather teased. And they all laughed out loud, even Jane Ann who did not understand yet what he was saying.

"I am Jane Ann," she said over and over several times, "Jane Ann," she repeated. Then pointing at Rena, she said "Rena" in Sioux and, pointing to Grandfather, she said "Grandfather" in Sioux.

Red Cloud laughed, "She wants to know my name," and he said it very carefully so she would understand. She repeated it back to him perfectly.

He could see that she was tired though, and so he bent his head once and turned to talk to Grandfather and Rena. The girl rested.

Red Cloud proceeded then to tell Grandfather about the celebration. "All afternoon, there will be eating and dancing. Sitting Bull has invited the white eyes Captain from Laramie where they are trying to build a fort, and he asked them to come with some of his men to see how our brave hunters have rescued a white girl." He paused with a gleam in his eye. "Do you think they will come?" he asked.

Grandfather shrugged, "Who knows?" was all he had to say about the matter. He wished Sitting Bull would be a little more careful about the white eyes. But he didn't want to say that in front of anyone. As far as he was concerned, Sitting Bull was a mighty warrior, an able chief, and a good friend. But where the white eyes were concerned, he could be like a little child standing too near the fire, trying too hard to please someone. Who knew better than this warrior in front of him that pleasing someone does not make them our friend?

Rena clapped her hands, "I will delight in every bite of the white buffalo cow you four mighty warriors brought in for us all." She leaned over close to Jane Ann. "Which also saved your life, and now it shall save ours. What a fine blessing you already are!"

Jane Ann could not exactly understand what Rena was talking about but she recognized it had something to do with her and so she smiled.

Jane Ann kept falling asleep and waking all the day, partly because of the sleeping medicine, and partly because of the healing going on. Finally during a long time awake, she tried to ask Rena about her Mama and Papa Rogers; however she could not get her to understand what she was saying. When Grandfather came back in the tipi, Jane Ann motioned to him over and over saying, "Papa, Papa, where is my Papa?" Then pointing to Rena, Jane Ann would say, "Mama, Mama, where is my Mama?" Neither Rena nor Grandfather understood exactly what she was asking of them. They were not too surprised when they saw tears streaming from her eyes again.

Rena sat beside her and attempted to soothe her by singing a lullaby that she often sang to the small children. It had a good affect because Jane Ann smiled again. Grandfather just wondered what she was asking and, for the first time, he wished that he understood the white eyes' language.

When the celebration was in full swing, it was a real surprise to many of the people to see a dozen or more of the white military all dressed up in their uniforms come riding cavalry style into camp. Of course, they all knew Sitting Bull had invited them; however, no one expected them to actually come. The eating and dancing paused just long enough for the people to open enough space for them to ride in. Of course, mothers gathered their children near to them out of fear they might be trampled by one of the cavalry horses. Grandfather spit on the ground and turned to go back into his tipi where Jane Ann and Rena were.

Rena was looking outside. She had opened the flap so she and Jane Ann could see the soldiers riding in. Jane Ann herself had never seen the cavalry before, Rena noticed by her reaction to them. Jane Ann had seen one or two soldiers in St. Louis, but not a whole double line of them like there were coming into Sitting Bull's camp.

Grandfather turned his back to the door of the tent, and to the soldiers. He slowly lit his pipe and just as slowly took a few puffs.

Jane Ann liked the way Grandfather's pipe smelled, and it almost drew her attention away from the lines of soldiers. There he sat, white haired ancient faced Indian gentleman, smoking his pipe as serenely as any English country gentleman. That is what Jane Ann was thinking as she watched Grandfather. She suddenly propped herself on one arm and reached over to pat Grandfather's arm.

Grandfather smiled. He thought she was trying to tell him not to worry that the soldiers would be leaving soon. He wondered if maybe she did not like the white eyes soldiers either. He could hear them when they finally stopped and got off their horses on the Captain's order. Of course, Grandfather could not understand their language either, but he knew the Captain's voice! He had heard it often enough ever since they started building the fort at Laramie. It was the stray soldier here and there that had been causing so much trouble.

Rain came running into the tipi breathless with excitement. He pulled up short and dropped into a squat on the floor beside Grandfather. His heart was beating a mile a minute with excitement more than from the run over to the tipi. He was talking to Grandfather and looking at the red-haired girl. He had not seen her with her eyes open. They were as blue as the early morning sky just as Red Cloud had said. Maybe they were light blue as two bluebell flowers. But, no, they were as dark as the evening sky. She had a pretty smile! He grinned at her and she smiled again.

Rain asked Rena and Grandfather if the girl was alright. They both assured him she was going to be, and then they gave him a quick explanation of her injuries although Grandfather was sure that Rain was not listening to them at all, but staring at the girl.

"Jane Ann," the girl repeated slowly and deliberately to Rain. "I am" and she pointed to herself, "Jane Ann." He understood!

"Rain," he repeated pointing to himself and repeating it again. She understood and she smiled at him again.

"She has a very beautiful smile," Rain said to nobody in particular. Rena laughed and Grandfather snorted.

Jane Ann was watching Rain. Perhaps, Jane Ann thought, perhaps she was not supposed to see the lines of soldiers as they made themselves at home. Then, suddenly in a panic, she remembered Mama and Papa, and she started sobbing loudly. If the soldiers heard her, surely one of them would come to investigate and that person could talk to these wonderful people and ask them about her parents. Oh, if only someone would tell her!

Outside, however, no one could hear Jane Ann's crying because of the celebration noise and laughter going on. Grandfather suddenly stood up and, putting out his pipe, he hurried to stop Jane Ann from moving around and perhaps knocking the bandages off her broken ankle and hurt leg. Lucky for her they were well made and did not come off.

Rena tried as best as she could to soothe Jane Ann. She also tried to help Grandfather settle Jane Ann down. Neither of them could imagine what made her scream and cry like that. They also wished they could understand what she kept saying over and over, but they did not.

Rain was puzzled. At first, he had just stood up, but then he, too, tried to speak gently to the girl to help keep her from crying. Then he finally had stood frozen and helpless, that is, until Red Cloud came walking in with a large portion of buffalo and everything else to eat that had been served around the campfire.

Red Cloud walked over and placed the plate of food beside Jane Ann. "Eat." was all he said, then he repeated it once even though he could tell right away that she had been crying. He turned to Grandfather. "Is she in pain again?" he asked.

Grandfather shook his head. "No, I did not think so, but maybe she is. She will be in far worse pain though if she continues to thrash around like that and happens to disturb the bandage holding her ankle bones together.

She keeps asking for something but we do not know what it is." He just shook his head and motioned for Jane Ann to shush and lie still.

Rena was so touched by Jane Ann's agitation that she determined she would find out somehow what it was that she wanted.

When Jane Ann opened her eyes again, Rena was still sitting there beside her. Jane Ann knew she was safe. Something about the woman was very comforting. Perhaps it was the soft and easy way she moved around the tipi, or the sound of her voice speaking so gently. She had been humming when Jane Ann opened her eyes again, and that particularly reminded her of her Mother. Jane Ann wished she could communicate better.

"Re-na," Jane Ann began trying again. She held up three fingers. One finger she pointed at herself and said, "Jane Ann." The second finger she pointed to one side of her and said, "Mama." The third finger she pointed to the other side of her and said, "Papa." There was a puzzled look on Rena's face, but she nodded slowly in agreement. Then Jane Ann tried again, this time by saying "Mama" and pointing to Rena, and then saying "Papa" as she pointed to the open flap leading outside the tipi where Grandfather was. Rena seemed to understand that. She got up and patted Jane Ann on the arm. Then she went outside.

This time she came back with Red Cloud. He had seen Rena walking around looking for someone (she told him for Grandfather), and he sent someone to find Grandfather for her. But he wanted to go back to see Jane Ann again. He had asked one of the soldiers from Fort Laramie about the words, "Mama and Papa" and the soldier had answered mostly in sign language that the words meant Mother and Father. Jane Ann was asking about her family! Red Cloud had wondered why a young girl would be traveling alone. It just made sense. She was asking about her Mother and Father. She had not been traveling alone.

Then Rena and Rain (who had joined them again) began talking at once. Rena picked up a blanket and, folding it in a ball she began cradling it in her arms while rocking back and forth, all the while saying "Ma-ma" as Jane had said it.

Jane Ann nodded vigorously. She pulled herself to a halfway sitting position to watch all three of them.

Rain stood holding a pretend gun while saying "bang" and then "Papa."

Jane Ann nodded and smiled. She was thinking how funny it will be when Rain finds out Papa could not even shoot a gun, that he did not even have any bullets to practice with.

Rena grabbed a handful of the packed down snow from outside and showed Jane Ann. She drew pictures with her hands. High mountain, snow falling, everyone gone, Mama no more, Papa no more, Jane Ann covered by white buffalo and the snow.

Jane Ann sighed a deep painful sigh. Somehow she had known Mama and Papa were gone. But, what if they had been saved by someone else as she was saved by the hunting party, and they had not known she was here? She sobbed loudly again. Rena and the young men let her cry as they sat helplessly watching her, knowing that now she understood they had not found anyone but her.

Jane Ann realized suddenly the Spirit people were present with them. Clearly she could see the Indian woman in white who had saved her, the one who had brought all the others to reassure her she would be alright. She watched her bring Mama and Papa to say they loved her and would always be with her when she needed them. Then her own Mother, Dorothy, who always brought the lavender smell, and then the Grandmothers gathered with them, and then others Jane Ann did not know. Here they were again walking easily about among the little group inside the tipi.

As Jane Ann looked and watched the spirit people, her tear stained face began to smile and a glow shone around her. She had no more tears, and no more sobbing and calling aloud. Jane Ann could see all her loved ones, as well as the lady in white very clearly.

Jane Ann suddenly leaned back and sighed. She appeared to Rena and Red Cloud and Rain to be looking into some invisible world and she had a look on her face like a medicine person does when he is communing with the Spirits. Then she began whispering as if to some unseen person, and finally she turned to Rena, Red Cloud and Rain.

"It's alright now. I know, I remember where Mama and Papa are. I thank you for being so kind." Jane Ann whispered to those watching her. "They are alright, they are in heaven with Mother Rogers and all our relatives." Then she added, "White Buffalo Woman told me."

They looked at Jane and at each other. Whatever it was that had happened, Rena could not wait to talk to Grandfather about it. When she did later, Grandfather said Jane Ann was probably communicating with the spirits of those she was asking about. Rena had looked at Jane Ann differently after that. How could a girl who was not a Sioux, not a native peoples of any name, how could she have a gift so rare and good, one that was honored by all native peoples? Perhaps Grandfather had been right and there was only one Great Spirit of all peoples in the whole earth no matter where they were born or how they look, no matter to which peoples they belong.

In the following weeks, while Jane Ann's ankle and leg were healing, Red Cloud and Rain came often to her tent. As she grew stronger, both of them began taking turns lifting her from the mat and taking her out into the sunlight. Even with the snow on the ground, it felt good to Jane Ann to be in the sunlight.

She began to be comfortable sitting for a long time watching the children playing, looking at the women as they went about their duties whether it was preparing the evening meal or getting an animal skin ready for drying. Or while sewing. Jane Ann began to learn more of the Sioux language. The children helped her most with the language. Perhaps they taught her as they were taught, but whatever term or new word she learned from the children was never forgotten by Jane Ann.

Jane Ann never tired of watching Rena either. She carried healing potions from tipi to tipi around the camp, anytime she was called she would get out Grandfather's bowl and pestle and grind some herbs or roots together, and off she would go. As Jane Ann watched Rena, she observed how happy and joyful she seemed. Her life could not be easy and yet she always smiled at everyone. Even when she thought she was alone and not being observed by anyone, Jane Ann had caught her with a smile on her face or sometimes humming a happy melody.

Jane Ann remembered Mama as being a very happy person, and Papa, too. They both made light of somber and sad things, Jane Ann had always thought that was because of her, but maybe that really had been their nature, too. Accept what comes and turn it into a happy adventure. If she could learn one thing from the two of them, she hoped it would be to do just that.

Grandfather and Rena still would not let her stand on her legs. From her growing understanding of the Sioux language, Jane Ann was able to see they were worried she might never be able to walk again. It was difficult for Jane Ann not to cry when she thought about not walking and not running anymore. The only way was to keep remembering that life is an adventure, at every turn there is something new. She was alive, and that was something she was thankful for. She was among good people, and that was something she was certainly grateful for. It was winter and cold, yet someone cared enough to make sure she was warm enough, safe, and fed often. When she began to consider all her blessings, she dared not begin to grieve over not being able to walk again yet!

One afternoon, Red Cloud and Rain came to get Jane Ann and they brought her out into the camp. It was nearing the end of winter. She knew that by the way the snow was getting thinner and thinner on the ground. Oh, it was still cold, but not the bitter blowing wind cold it had been. She snuggled her soft blanket around her shoulders and Rain tucked it around her legs. Red Cloud and Rain sat down also, and Red Cloud took out a flute and began playing a beautiful melody.

Soon the others who had first found her joined their circle. Grandfather also came and Rena, too. Each one brought sticks of wood with them and piled them on the center of their growing circle of people. By then, Left Hand and Right Hand had joined their circle, so now all the hunters who had found her were there. Rena and other women began passing around cups of warm soothing tea and Jane Ann accepted hers gratefully. ("One day," Jane Ann was thinking, "I will walk around a circle where you are sitting and serve you tea.") Rena's eyes were sparkling as she handed Jane Ann's cup to her. The afternoon began joyfully and continued for a long time.

Each of the hunters who had found Jane Ann two years before in the snow then, in turn, stood and described what they had seen and heard on the day White Buffalo Woman had shown them where to find the biggest buffalo cow they had ever seen, and the girl they each pointed to with a smile, Jane Ann! All around the circle grew as many people came to join in and hear what was going on. They all remembered the delicious taste of buffalo meat. They were showing their approval with calls and yodels and hitting sticks on the ground.

Then Rena and Grandfather both nodded at Jane Ann to speak. When she tried to stand as the others were doing when they spoke, Grandfather shook his head. Instead, he stood and easily lifted her and turned so all in the circle could see her as she spoke.

"I thank you, brave warriors," Jane Ann began in flawless Sioux, "for finding me and bringing me to such good people. I am grateful for your kindness and your care. I thank you for making me feel so much at home." That was about all she could think of to say. She could have said more in English, but she wanted to speak so all could hear and understand in their own language.

Grandfather was smiling. Rena was smiling and clucking her tongue. Jane Ann could hear the yodels and calls from far back in the growing crowd. Then suddenly another seemed to suddenly appear standing beside her and Grandfather. He was not as tall as Grandfather, his face was not as thin or wizened. He had a big nose and a wide face, high cheek bones, and thin lips. His hands were very big, Jane Ann noticed as he held up one hand in greeting. He had a sad twinkle in his eyes like a dreamer who is unable to describe his dream.

"Ah, ho, welcome, Sitting Bull, Chief of the Sioux Nation," Grandfather was grinning from ear to ear.

"Ah, ho, friend Grandfather," Sitting Bull nodded. Then, "Is this our visitor from a foreign land?" He was looking at Jane Ann.

"Yes," Grandfather said.

"Put her down again, Grandfather, and I will sit with you." Sitting Bull was already being offered a cup of tea by Rena and one of the other women came immediately to spread a blanket for Chief Sitting Bull to sit on beside them.

"I am happy to be asked to join you today." Sitting Bull nodded to Grandfather and Jane Ann. "We are honored to have you here and happy that White Buffalo Woman has so honored us." Sitting Bull paused and watched Jane Ann's expression.

Jane Ann was happy, too, and smiling as she nodded again and again. She noticed that Sitting Bull had on a red shirt and a heavy coat made of some kind of skins that were a beautiful gray color, and pants made of the same soft material as Grandfather wore. She had thought from her children's books that chiefs always wore headdresses made of feathers, but

Sitting Bull had a cloth band tied around his head with feathers sticking up from one side. Later, when Jane Ann asked Rena about the feather head dress she had seen in her books in England, Rena nodded and told her that all chiefs have one made especially for them to wear at big ceremonies.

Jane Ann could tell that Chief Sitting Bull appeared to be near what Papa's age had been. As she watched him talking, she thought about the gatherings in Papa's den when the men would smoke cigars or pipes and talk politics or about what was happening in the "new world." Now here she was, not too long after her sixteenth birthday, watching the Chief of the Sioux Nation speak quietly to his people, and to her and all the women in the crowd equally with the men.

"Jane Ann," she heard him and she came out of her reverie, "Will you tell us about your journey and how you came to be where you were found in the snow under the buffalo many months ago?" Many in the crowd wanted to hear her story.

"Just talk to Sitting Bull," Grandfather whispered to her.

Jane Ann could feel Rena pat her hand. She took courage knowing she could do it. "Sir, my family and I came by ship from our home in the countryside near London in the country of England." She paused to see if he was understanding her, and he smiled and gestured for her to go on. "Then we came by train to St. Louis where Papa got a covered wagon and supplies for us. And then we set out for California." At that word which she spoke in English because she did not know what it was in Sioux, there were murmurs of wonder through the crowd. Many of them knew about California and the rush of white people going to dig for gold.

Sitting Bull only nodded. He, too, knew what she was saying.

She continued on. "On our drive across to where you found me, we only saw one group of people, and they were Indians called Kickapoo." She looked at Grandfather who was listening intently. He motioned for her to continue talking to Sitting Bull.

"We could not talk to the Kickapoo very well because we did not know their language and Papa could only guess at what they were saying." Jane Ann told them how the Kickapoo ate supper with them, and then later came back and took most of the food they had for their trip. "Papa had guns but the man in the shop failed to give us bullets for the guns. We did alright for food awhile and when we began to be short of food, Papa assured Mama and me we would find some Army post or trading post and stop and replenish everything we needed."

At that point, Chief Sitting Bull breathed a deep sigh.

Jane Ann chose her words carefully, hoping it was alright to tell them. "At supper one evening, I had a headache and I know that the Spirit people always come and show me things when I have a headache." She paused but no one was stopping her yet. "They showed me white snow falling down in an avalanche burying our covered wagon and us under massive amounts of snow. I was scared but Papa said we weren't going into any mountains. I had already heard he and Mama talking about the guide giving us the wrong directions, and how we could find help to get to the Mississippi River and go on a steamboat around Mexico to go to California." She drew in a deep breath and then recalled Papa had been so hopeful. Oh, how she missed Papa and Mama!

"Then what happened?" Rena was patting her hand and whispering.

"The next thing I woke being in the snow so white it was hard to see anything at all. Papa said we might be lost and he tried hard to find a way out, but the avalanche came and buried us. That's all I remember until I saw the Lady dressed in White showing me Mama and Papa, and all my real relatives. The Lady in White promised I would be alright, that someone would find me, that Mama and Papa would be with me when I needed them. Oh, but I was hoping they would be found, too!" She took another deep breath and continued. "The rest you know. Red Cloud, Left Hand, Rain, Right Hand, they found the buffalo cow and me under it still alive. I don't know how I got there or how the buffalo cow got there either. Maybe she was caught in the avalanche, too. Maybe the Lady in white did it. I don't know really. But I am grateful anyway. And, I am grateful to the brave hunters who found me!" She stopped talking and waited.

After a pause, Chief Sitting Bull spoke, but again, it seemed he was speaking to her alone. "Jane Ann, I will give you an Indian name. From this day you will be called White Buffalo Woman. She told our brave hunters where to find you. Perhaps she means for you to be a blessing in many ways to our People but also for you and your people as well." He paused. "I go away hunting before dawn. When I return, will you, and Rena and Grandfather sit with me around my fire? I want to know more about your people and about the place where you come from." He looked at each of them. "Will you do this?"

Jane Ann nodded and said, "Yes, I will be happy to sit at your fire and answer your questions. Thank you for inviting me."

Grandfather and Rena agreed it would be good. Grandfather wished Sitting Bull and his braves a good hunt, and ended with, "We will sit together around your fire when you return."

Sitting Bull stood and walked away as quietly as he had appeared. The others stood and moved back as he walked through. Red Cloud began to play his flute again, and Jane Ann sat watching him. Soon almost everyone else had left to go to their own tipi except for Jane Ann and Red Cloud and Grandfather. Even Rain, Left Hand and Right Hand had gone.

When Red Cloud finished playing his flute, he put it away, but not before Jane Ann had told him how beautiful the music was. That seemed to please him.

CHAPTER 9

As Jane Ann went to sleep that evening, she wished she had her charcoal and drawing paper. Maybe she could ask Grandfather to have someone get her some from the Laramie Fort. She wished she had her journal, too. It had been two years since she had written in it, and now she had a good deal to say that would be very interesting to share with George and Georgette someday. Oh, well, all her things were buried deep under the snow on the mountain.

The next morning Red Cloud called a soft greeting from outside the tipi to Jane Ann and Rena. He said he had brought Jane Ann a gift, and that he was leaving with Sitting Bull and the other braves. He added quietly, "I will see you when we return."

Within a few minutes, they heard the braves mounting their horses outside camp and almost without a whisper of noise they were gone. Rena looked outside to see what Red Cloud had left for Jane Ann. Carefully she brought it in so the girl could see.

"It's a walking stick!" Jane Ann chuckled. "When did he make it, I wonder?" for she knew he was at the gathering at the campfire with her the day before. When would he have had time?

A cough alerted the ladies that Grandfather was coming into the tipi with firewood to start the fire. Soon they were sharing an early morning bite to eat and the warm tea that always made Jane Ann feel cozy and safe.

Jane Ann was wondering when she would ever walk again. Or if she would ever be able to go look for her charcoals and paints and paper, for her journal, for whatever may still be there under the snow with Mama's and Papa's remains.

Grandfather could tell Jane Ann was deep in thought. "Hi, ho," he began, "That is a fine walking stick you have there from Red Cloud"

"Yes," Jane Ann agreed, "He has carved and smoothed the wood until it is a comfortable thing to touch and a beautiful thing to see. I just wonder how he had the time to do such beautiful work. It's a puzzle to me."

"Ho," Rena agreed, "And so it would be for us if we did not know about the stick already. Would you like Grandfather to tell you the story?"

Jane nodded. "Of course, please, I want to hear the story."

"Well," Grandfather began, "Some years ago Red Cloud went with a raiding party of Lakota Sioux to steal some Crow ponies from their camp. He got in a fight with one of them and the Crow shot him in the foot. Of course, Red Cloud continued fighting and killed the Crow honorably. When he came back to camp, we doctored his foot as good as we could, but I'll have to say, I looked at it and figured he would never walk again."

Rena nodded. "Yes, it was a bad injury. The bullet had torn through the center of his foot shattering all the bones and tearing the tendons. I didn't believe he would ever be able to straighten his foot in the right way again to walk and run."

"But," Grandfather continued, "He would shake his head and insist that he would be hunting with his friends before mid-Spring that year, even though we both insisted that would be impossible." Grandfather shook his head and smiled. "He is a headstrong man. He takes time to make his mind up, but when it is made up to do something, he does it."

"Yes," Rena nodded. Then she looked at Jane Ann who was listening intently to every word. "Jane Ann, Red Cloud used that walking stick for a long time until one day he just put it down and went hunting with the others."

Jane Ann nodded and smiled. She wasn't surprised.

"Yep," Grandfather continued, "Maybe Red Cloud knows something we don't know yet."

"What's that, Grandfather?" Jane Ann asked.

"Maybe the mind is the power, the strength, for the body." He looked at her carefully. "Have you noticed Red Cloud's limp?"

Jane Ann had noticed. She had thought about it and wondered several times if it was really a limp or just something she was imagining. He had a definite way of walking that was different from the others. It appeared to be a sure steady gait but it had a pause in it.

"I have" Jane Ann nodded, "but I thought it might be my imagination."

"Or perhaps because of his long legs or his being so tall?" Rena added with a laugh, "He is certainly a head taller than most Sioux."

"Why would he give me his stick?" Jane Ann wondered aloud.

"Maybe," Grandfather said slowly, "because you have a wounded foot, too, and it will help you walk when you can stand up again?" He watched her carefully. "Maybe because you are his friend?"

Rena laughed. "You two have to have reasons for everything!" She got up, "Look at the light in the morning sky. Soon it will be Spring and all the flowers will be blossoming, their sweet perfume filling the air, and you, Jane Ann will walk and run and be happy and blossom, too!"

Grandfather nodded but he was afraid in his heart that Jane Ann would never walk again, even if she took heart from the story about Red Cloud, but because her ankle was hurt so bad. Crushed bones are hard to put right, and the ankle is the main support which allows us to walk and run. "You are not ready for the stick yet," Grandfather said, "Soon you will be. In the meantime, Rena and I will change the covering on your ankle and see how well it is healing."

Rena already had the water warm and the little bowl of herbal medicines ready for the wound. Grandfather had brought in strong sticks of wood which were cut and shaped in just the right way to be a support and protection over the new bandage.

They found her deeply cut leg was now well healed but there would remain a long scar to remind her or anyone who could see her leg that some terrible thing had happened to her. Rena was glad dresses were worn long so Jane Ann would not care about how it looked.

The ankle was still very fragile looking. The cuts that were sutured had healed but the bones were still healing.

"Sometimes," Grandfather explained, "Bones take many months, as much as a year when they are crushed, to heal properly. We must all be patient. You must be the most patient." Grandfather nodded toward Jane Ann, "You must not be in a hurry to stand up or to walk and run. Heal first! Will you be patient?"

Only if I can have some paper and charcoal or something to draw with." She told him. Then she looked at Rena, "I can be content with just sitting if I can do something I love like drawing and painting." She hoped they understood.

Rena knew Rain sometimes talked about the drawings he had seen one time at the trading post. Rena herself had helped make paints for one of their people who drew pictures on stones and tree bark one whole year long. That same woman later had taught many of the children how to draw and paint. Rena smiled as she remembered that was a very good summer for them all. "We can get you paints and charcoal," Rena said, "Rain can help us get tree bark and dry it, maybe he can even go to the trading post and get real paper!"

Jane Ann was beginning to feel everything was going to be alright. She would be able to draw again. There were so many faces she wanted to put on paper! So many wonderful sights she would like to remember forever and to share with others. Maybe one day she would see Uncle Percy and Aunt Agnes and show them the drawings of all the people who had been so kind to her after Mama and Papa had died.

"Yes, yes." Jane Ann kept saying over and over to herself. She did not even bother trying to see her leg. It felt better. She did not doubt that she was going to be able to walk and run someday. And just think! Red Cloud had gone through the same thing, a terrible wounded foot! And look at him now!

Rain wandered back to camp later that morning and looked for Rena and Jane Ann or Grandfather. He wanted Jane Ann to know that he had gone back to the Black Hills and dug around some more, looking for anything from Papa's covered wagon.

"Everything must still be buried very deep," he told Jane Ann carefully, "You can be sure the Great Spirit would not let your folks suffer. They are in the Spirit world right now looking at you!" He patted her arm.

Jane Ann nodded. "I know but I thank you for looking anyway." She would always remember how Mama and Papa were before they died in the avalanche, and also what beautiful and peaceful spirits they were in the spirit world beyond She was so glad they had appeared to her so she would know and not wonder about them; however, for Rain to go and dig to see if he could find them was a kind and thoughtful act she would appreciate forever.

"I heard Red Cloud gave you his stick!" Rain said suddenly.

"Yes, and it is beautiful." She was eager to talk about her gift. "How kind of him to give it to me to use. That gives me hope to believe I will walk again and not a long time away. Did you know he was going to give it to me?" Jane asked Rain.

Rain shook his head. "Nope, I thought he had thrown it away long ago! Then I saw him whittling it down so it would not be too hard for you to use, and that's when I figured he was going to give it to you."

Rena and Grandfather joined them, and they all began to talk about the snows melting sooner than expected. They were not all melted away yet, but soon would be. Spring always brought joy with it.

"Rain," Rena said, "Will you be going to the white man's trading post again?"

Rain nodded. "I can if you have a reason for me to go get something."

"It's for Jane Ann," Rena explained, "She would like to have drawing things if you can find them."

"Yes," Jane Ann added, "Paper, charcoal, any kind of paints, anything that I can use to draw faces and scenes with would be very good."

Rain didn't understand at first but finally did when Jane Ann talked about drawing faces, "Yes, I saw some drawings of faces at the trading post last year. Some white man traveling through was drawing faces of Indians He wanted to draw mine but I would have to stay there overnight, and I didn't want to." He shook his head remembering that he had not trusted the white man either, he even doubted the drawings were done by the man that had them. "I didn't actually see that man doing the drawing. But I know what you mean." He paused and then, "When do you want me to go, Rena?"

Grandfather spoke up, "We can maybe take Jane Ann if we wait a few more weeks. By then it will be better weather." He added, "Her leg will be better then, too."

"I can wait awhile more, I guess," Jane Ann nodded as she was trying not to be disappointed.

"How about the bark and the charcoal from the hills?" Rena asked no one in particular. "Remember when Little Dove was drawing pictures and taught the children that year how to draw? Remember Cross Eyes dried bark until he said it was like the white eyes paper?" Rena continued, "Someone got charcoal from the hills? Remember?"

Rain slapped his hand on his thigh. "I do remember, I was little but I remember that was the year Little Dove had a baby."

Rena nodded. "All the children tried to draw pictures of Little Dove for a long time after she left us. We kept her pictures, the ones she drew on the bark, for awhile, but I don't know what happened to them."

Grandfather answered, "Her husband, Grey Owl, burned them." Then he added, "It was in a fit of grief that he threw the drawings into the fire."

Jane Ann was getting one of her headaches. That might mean she would see the Spirit people again. "I want to go back into the tipi and rest." She said suddenly.

Rain jumped up and picked her up, "I'll take you," he said, and he was glad to be doing something. He was thinking, "Melt, snows, melt, we want to get busy," as he carried her easily into her tipi and placed her on the sleeping mat.

"Thank you, Rain," Jane Ann spoke painfully, her headache worsening. "I think I will rest now and I will see you later."

He murmured something and left the tipi.

Later, Rena asked Jane Ann what had been wrong. She reluctantly told her about her headaches and seeing the Spirit people often when she had them. Grandfather came in and joined them and he listened intently as she described being hurt in a fall when she was three years old and afterwards having the headaches begin with the visions.

Grandfather spoke again, "Jane Ann, that is a gift of the Great Spirit to be honored." He could see her eyes opening wide looking at him. He continued, "Seeing the Spirit people is not a thing to hide among the Sioux, it is a great gift. Perhaps it is for this reason that we are invited to join Chief Sitting Bull around his fire. Maybe you are supposed to share your gift with the Sioux Nation. Perhaps that is why you are here with us now at this time of great change for our people."

Rena opened her mouth but then did not speak. Instead, she was thinking, "Yes, yes, that is it! The Spirit people have sent this English girl to us so we will know ahead of time what is going to happen." Then she spoke to Jane Ann quietly, "Do not hide your gift from us, Jane Ann, speak and tell us each time all the words given you to say to our people. You are really our Blessing!" Her heart was singing just to be a part of bringing help to her people.

So many native peoples from the East had been coming into Sioux land looking for help to fight the white man. For months they had come wounded and crippled and broken all because, Grandfather had been told, the white man wanted their land. Sitting Bull had sent small war parties at different times to help the larger groups who wandered in but he had hesitated when it was just a few or one or two wounded Indians. He would invite the few to "Come settle here with us where there is room." But, everybody wanted their own land and their own people.

Sitting Bull had attempted to talk to the white men who came into Sioux territory belong to the land and they are here to take from it and to give back to it life." But the white man had not listened. The latest insult was the attempt to build a fort at Laramie south of them, in the building then for over a year's time. Over and over they had brought in wagon loads of building supplies, and many soldiers came. However, the soldiers did not like the deserted area which only had a few Indians traveling about going to or from hunting, or young hunters out learning how to be brave warriors. Not a few times had the soldiers took it upon themselves to shoot at the Indians. Even if they did not shoot at them, they would laugh at them and make fun of how they looked and acted. Even the Indian peoples around the fort had begun to fight with each other more. Maybe it was because they had more guns available to them.

Sitting Bull had tried to talk to the cavalry captain at Laramie but he had not been willing to listen. Even Sitting Bull had been surprised when the Captain came and brought some of his cavalry to the celebration of the buffalo cow. But they had not stayed long. Only the Captain looked around the camp and when he could not determine the reason for the celebration, he called his men to leave. They were not friendly people.

Grandfather wanted to stay as far away from the white cavalry as possible because he had a very bad feeling about them. He was hoping, however, that this girl may have a warning that would guide the Sioux peoples into finding the right person to talk to in order to get the cavalry out of Sioux territory.

"You do not have to hide your gift from us," Grandfather assured Jane Ann. "Red Cloud, too, can hear the Spirit people as could his father."

Rena nodded. "Yes, and Grandfather can hear them, too." Then she added, "Don't be afraid, Jane Ann, please tell us what the Spirit people want you to say to us anytime you hear them or see them. Will you do this?"

Jane Ann nodded. It would be a relief to live openly with her abilities and to be able to talk about what she saw or heard at the time without fear of being made fun of or considered crazy. "Yes, I will, I promise!"

CHAPTER 10

Sitting Bull and Red Cloud, along with the rest of the hunting party, came back four days later. They brought back many animals ready to be skinned and used as food for the whole camp. The camp was preparing for another big celebration.

Jane Ann was beginning to feel like she was home with these peoples. Grandfather and Rena treated her as if she were their daughter, in the case of Grandfather maybe his great-granddaughter! Rain, Left Hand and Right Hand, and Red Cloud were her friends. Any of the girls her age and older with new babies had become her friends. There seemed not to be the line of family in the camp that she remembered in England. It seemed that everyone acted as if they were related in some way. The children appeared to be cared for and looked after by everyone equally, yet every child knew and returned to its own mother or father.

There were arguments. Jane Ann had seen one just recently when two young boys were wanting the same hunting knife. Jane Ann had watched and marveled at the way peace was made swiftly between the two. Just before then, Grandfather had brought Jane Ann out to help Rena wash some vegetables and cut them for the soup she was going to make for supper.

The two boys started pushing and shoving, and then their voices rose in anger. Grandfather had walked over and separated them. He had pointed to the sky and asked the boys in a stern but kind voice, "Who made the sun?" and both boys had answered "The Great Spirit." Then he had asked, "Who make the knife?" Both boys had shrugged their shoulders because they did not know. He gave them a moment to think, then he added, "Neither of you nor I can make the sun shine or hide its rays. Yet, each one of us can make our own knife. The sun shines on everyone of us equally, not just on our camp and not on our enemies' camp. Have you not considered that the Great One Who made the sun to shine equally on us all has given us already all that we need? Cannot either of you make his own knife? Cannot you find within your own self the same generosity of spirit that the Great One who made the sun has for us all?"

It was a lot to think about. But the boys made peace. One of them picked up the knife and offered it to the other. The other one refused but looked instead to a third boy and pointed that he should give him the knife. So it had been given to the boy whose father had made it. Then the two other boys who had been fighting went and asked their fathers to make them knives.

Grandfather said later that he wished it was as easy to convince the white man there was land enough for all and that no fighting should be done over that which already belongs to everyone. Jane Ann had agreed.

A boy came to where Jane Ann and Grandfather and Rena were and asked them to come to supper time at Sitting Bull's fire. Rena asked the boy to tell Chief Sitting Bull's wife that she would bring the vegetable soup that was cooking on their fire. She knew that his wife would want to serve the meat she had chosen for them.

The whole camp had been celebrating one way or another ever since Chief Sitting Bull and the others had returned with such an abundance of meat and skins. The men skinned the animals and the women cleaned them and prepared them to eat. All the while they worked, Jane Ann could hear laughing and singing and humming all around the camp, and it was a nice sound she hoped to remember always. The children ran around freely playing and they made such happy sounds, Jane Ann would remember them always, too.

She wondered where Red Cloud was. As she watched the people around where she was sitting, and as far as she could see around the camp, Jane Ann looked for Red Cloud. Something about him bringing his walking stick to her the other morning had touched her and she wanted to thank him. But, he was nowhere she could see. She wished for the first time she could run to where he was or at least walk and go look for him.

Jane Ann suddenly realized how blue she was feeling, and that usually meant a headache was coming. She wondered if she should ask to be excused from going with Rena and Grandfather to Chief Sitting Bull's campfire, or if she should go and see what happens.

As if Grandfather could read her thoughts, he leaned over and whispered, "You could not choose a better time than this evening to hear the Spirit people." Then he patted her arm and said, "Chief Sitting Bull will be listening well, and so will Red Cloud."

Jane Ann smiled and nodded. She was glad Grandfather was going to be with her.

Sure enough, her headache came swiftly and all afternoon she struggled not to see or hear the Spirit world. Just to wait until they sat around the fire or at least until they were with Chief Sitting Bull. For some reason Grandfather had not indicated, it seemed important that Sitting Bull hear what the Spirit people told her especially if it was about the Sioux Nation, or about the land, or about the white man coming into their land. For that reason, she asked to be taken back to their tipi.

Rain and Red Cloud came up about the time Grandfather was going to lift her up. Quickly Red Cloud reached for her first as, at the same time, he was greeting Grandfather and Rena with a "Hi ho!"

"Carry her gently for she has a painful headache." Rena called. "Take her to the tipi please."

Rain watched Red Cloud walk away with her and he wondered if he should follow and tell her he had been drying some bark for her to draw on. He decided to wait until later.

"When do you think Jane Ann's leg will be well enough for her to use the walking stick?" Rain asked Grandfather.

"Maybe not for awhile yet." Grandfather answered.

"How are we going to take her to the trading post then if she cannot walk?" he asked them.

Rena and Grandfather looked at each other. Both were thinking that maybe Jane Ann might never be able to walk again. They had not wanted to say it out loud though.

Grandfather spoke first, "We will take her on a travois and it will be a good trip for us." He said to Rain. Rena and Rain nodded agreement.

As they neared the tipi, Jane asked Red Cloud if they could sit for awhile and he placed her in a comfortable spot and sat down beside her. They sat quietly for a moment looking out over the camp and listening to the people talking and laughing.

Jane Ann wondered why she was suddenly so self-conscious. She owed her very life to this man yet she found it hard to speak her heart to him. It didn't make sense.

"I want to thank you," she began stuttering and wondering if her memory of the language would fail her, "for the walking stick, it is beautiful!" She watched his face.

He bent his head. Then he nodded and looked her in the eyes. Such beautiful blue eyes, like the bluebell flowers that bloom in Spring. Her voice was like the wind, a hushed whisper that was soothing and comforting. He wondered what his days would be like without this girl around to look at and do small things for. He had found out on a recent hunting trip with Chief Sitting Bull. He could not imagine her ever leaving their people. Because of his strong feelings, he knew that he must talk to Grandfather and Rena. But for now, in this moment, he listened to her intently as she spoke.

"Red Cloud, I do not want to embarrass you around Chief Sitting Bull's fire this evening, so I must tell you something before we go there." Her head was hurting bad. It always hurt when she was trying to suppress the images and voices. She was dizzy, too, and that was something new to add to her list of physical ailments! Perhaps it was that which made her cry, but cry she did, and she began sobbing like a little girl. Then she felt horrible about doing it.

Red Cloud lifted her easily and took her into the tipi. Then as she tried to speak and explain what was happening to her, he simply patted her hand and turned to leave, thinking surely he must have said or done something to offend her. Then he remembered that Rena had told him Jane Ann had a headache. So, as he put Jane Ann down, he patted her hand, and then turning, he left the tipi. Red Cloud walked back to where Rain and the others were. He could only wonder for now about this white girl who cried so easily, she who held his heart in her hands. He was sure now that he loved her.

By the time that Grandfather, Rena and Jane Ann had joined the circle around Sitting Bull's fire that evening, Jane Ann had forgotten her anxiety over crying and making Red Cloud feel embarrassed and uneasy around her. Instead, she was relaxing into the scenes that White Buffalo Woman was showing her.

Immediately, when she was put down on the blanket in the gathering circle, she was told to speak what she was seeing. She didn't know whose voice told her, but she could not have kept from it any longer anyway.

"White Buffalo Woman is pointing to a place near the white man's fort built at Laramie. She is showing me Red Cloud and some warriors going in peace to talk to the head of the white cavalry there. Some other Army men are riding in from another direction headed for the same place. They attack Red Cloud and his men," at that point her heart skipped and her voice faltered as she feared she was going to see him hurt or killed. Then she felt Grandfather squeeze her arm. She continued, "In the battle, a number of the white soldiers are killed, and she is showing me bodies lying on the ground, I think she is saying the number is 19. Red Cloud did not intend this to happen. He was attacked first and he had to fight or be killed." She stopped.

A few around the fire began to murmur and feel uneasy. To be watching a white girl with red hair telling them what White Buffalo Woman was showing her was a surprise to many of them. Some of them who did not know her were wondering why White Buffalo Woman would choose her to speak to them. Why would she be seeing a battle involving Sioux and white soldiers? Yet, those who knew her best believed that White Buffalo Woman had chosen the clearest channel to warn the Sioux people about the future. No one could have spoken clearer than Jane Ann did that evening.

"A strong current of fear and anger will grow as the story is told around campfire after campfire until, from those few who hate our people, there will come an order to kill us all or move us into small areas where we will be under the authority of the cavalry and the government. Within one year of the incident near Laramie, a troop of soldiers will march into a Sioux camp and murder over a hundred Sioux men, women and children, and their chief will be put in chains in prison." Jane Ann stopped. She was speaking in perfect Sioux even though she did not know all the language, but, at the same time, she was understanding it all in her own English language. Even as she described what she was seeing, she was also feeling the terror of the people. Jane Ann shivered.

Then she continued, "Listen well, there will be more and more white people coming to our land and we will have less and less freedom to move around. First, though, there will be a great war fought in the East between the white man in the North and the whites in the southern part of the Country. White Buffalo Woman says to watch for the end of that war. That will signal the inflow of many whites into our land and even farther to the big ocean. The Sioux will not be free to walk the land anymore. Only if the Sioux and all the other Indians find a language of peace to speak, and then only if the hearts of the white men are turned to peace, only then can there be a coming together. It will be a hard road to walk."

Jane Ann drew in a long breath. "In the years to come, Red Cloud will learn to talk to the white man, but even he will be deceived. Chief Sitting Bull, too, will reach out to the white man in peace, but he, as well, will be deceived. Watch out especially for a young man with white hair who claims to carry the symbol of peace. He will come to Sioux land with many cavalry. The destiny of the Sioux may be bound up in the destiny of this man. Be aware and watch for him after the whites finish warring with one another back East."

Jane Ann sighed, and she knew that was the end of White Buffalo Woman's message. She could not remember all she had said but she looked around at the faces and realized not a person was untouched by the message.

Grandfather and Rena sat with tears in their eyes.

Quietly they had all sat there, some eating, some passing around the plates of delicious food. Jane Ann was not hungry but she gladly drank the steaming tea and finally tasted the vegetables from Rena's soup. Politely she accepted bits of meat and was pleased to find it to be turkey or chicken, but she refused any more with gratitude. Occasionally she would look out the corner of her eye and see one of them looking at her.

She could only wonder where Red Cloud was. Right then she felt she had to speak to him, and explain herself to him, so he would understand why she cried earlier when he had been with her outside the tipi. She didn't know herself why she had cried then but she had to explain to him anyway Oh, if he were here, she wondered how awful he thought she must be to talk about his people and such awful things to see. It was too dark for Jane Ann to see anyone clearly who was not sitting close to the fire. She wondered where Red Cloud was.

Sitting Bull spoke privately to Jane Ann before Grandfather and Rena were to take her back to the tipi. "When was the first time White Buffalo Woman spoke to you?" Sitting Bull asked her.

"Back in England when I was a little girl, I think I was three years old." She replied. Then, "Here before the snowfall in the mountain," Jane Ann answered easily, "when Mama and Papa and I were traveling in the wagon on the way here, she warned me to tell them about the snow and the avalanche going to happen."

"And the next time?" Sitting Bull asked Jane.

"When I woke in the dark after the avalanche, I was so afraid and I thought I was dead because I could not feel my body or anything, and I couldn't see any light. Then she came and told me not to be afraid, that I would be safe, that someone would come for me soon, and that I should go with them. She showed me Mama and Papa and other relatives in the Spirit world. Then she helped me sleep until Red Cloud and Rain and the others found me." She shivered at remembering being buried in the snow, and the warm body of the dying buffalo cow.

"Will she come again to you?" Sitting Bull asked calmly as he watched Jane Ann.

"I guess she will, I don't know, I've never asked any of the Spirit people if or when they will come again." Then suddenly she remembered, "But my mother, Dorothy, I've asked her to come back but she never speaks, but just once, she just hugs me or touches my face and I feel better." Then she added, "My Mother just comes when I am scared, and I think maybe Mama and Papa may do that soon, too." Of course, she knew he wanted to know when White Buffalo Woman would come with messages again. "Oh, I wish I could tell you when White Buffalo Woman will speak again, but I can't! I'm afraid I don't know when!" She felt suddenly like such a silly girl anyway. Nobody had ever thought the visions were anything important except Mama and Papa, but they had not encouraged her. When the visions came, they just came with a banging headache. She just did not know what to say to Chief Sitting Bull.

However, Sitting Bull assured her, and later so did Grandfather and Rena, that he thought that, indeed, White Buffalo Woman had been speaking through Jane Ann. He teased her about being their peoples' blessing again.

But there were some present around that campfire who wondered what kind of cruel trick would bring a white girl to the camp of a Sioux chief. Some were concerned that it could be a cruel trick of the white man's, or else it could be just a silly young girl's made up stories.

Red Cloud was gone the next morning. Rain was gone, too. Rain left behind, just outside Jane Ann's tipi door flap, the bark he had been drying for her to draw on, and the charcoal he had found hidden deep in a cave in the Black Hills. Rena brought them in for Jane Ann to see, and then she left. Jane Ann was delighted with the bark and charcoal. At last, she would be able to draw again.

Jane Ann would have given anything to tell Red Cloud how sorry she was to have made him angry or offended him the day before. She wondered if he had heard by now what White Buffalo Woman had said about him. She wondered what he thought about her having such a gift and suddenly she decided she just didn't want the gift anymore. But that would be a neat trick. She had already learned that she could not simply will it away. Want it or not, she had visions again and again since she was three years old.

Sometimes Jane Ann also wished she had never climbed up to look at the sunlight in London that day, that she had never fallen down, and that she had never ended up at Uncle Percy's house. At the thought of Percy and Agnes she started crying. She wondered if they even knew about Mama and Papa being killed. Or if they knew she was here in a Sioux camp unable to walk or get around by herself. Of course they did not! She began to sob harder and harder. Right then, if she could have walked, she would have found a way to run as far as she could from Sitting Bull's camp and to never come back. It was just horrible to think she was the voice through which any peoples would learn about the horrors facing them.

"Oh, please, God," Jane Ann cried, "Please, please help me!"

She did not know how long she lay crying like a baby, but it must have been a long time. Neither Grandfather nor Rena came to comfort her. She even felt that she did not deserve comforting. What could either of them say to her anyway? Finally she cried herself to sleep and she hoped, as she was dropping off into sleep, that she slept until she could get up and run fast away from that place!

CHAPTER 11

Jane Ann awoke from sleep, and still no one had come to see about her. Neither Grandfather nor Rena. That's when she decided she would leave. It might not be easy, but it would be better than her staying where nobody could look her in the eyes anymore, where children and young people would begin to lose heart because of the awful things she told them that White Buffalo Woman had said. Who wanted to hear about fighting and being killed? She had been such a fool to speak aloud in front of the people!

Oh, Jane Ann thought, she really despised everything she had said the evening before while being with them around Sitting Bull's campfire. He must hate her and she wondered why he didn't kill her right there before everyone! He could have done it easily. She was not too sure if the roles had been reversed and Sitting Bull had been in her home in England saying awful things about England being taken over and many people being killed, that she wouldn't have killed him! Then she shook her head in disbelief that she would even think about such a thing! She quickly asked forgiveness.

Then she crawled over to the walking stick and made herself get up off the floor. She was determined that she was never going to be helpless again unless it were to sleep very short naps. She just wanted to be upright, standing up! It took her awhile and some perspiration to get on her feet. She was dizzy, but soon the dizziness would pass. Then she found herself becoming more and more sure she could walk with the stick! She could get away!

She gathered everything she thought she would need and stuffed it all in her pockets, including the pieces of dried bark (her "paper" Rain had made) and the charcoal. Also, of course, bits of food that she could find, and a knife.

It was slow going, but she hopped and held on, and she tried and kept trying until she was outside. She pulled herself in a direction that took her around the tent and into a small clearing back of the camp. She hoped she could leave the camp from that direction. When she sighted some horses tethered nearby, she lured one of them to her with a bit of raw carrot she had in her pocket.

She had to do a lot of strong pulling and pulling, but the horse was patient, and finally she got up and astride the animal. It was then she wondered what she could do to hold on to the walking stick. The idea then came to her to tie it to her back with a sash she had on her jacket. It worked and she set out on horseback not knowing which direction or even where she was heading.

Occasionally through the day she watched where the sun was and by doing so she could guess the time fairly well until she rode through the thick forest of trees. Doing that twice scared her so that she was determined not to go through a forest again, or even through what seemed like a few clumps of trees anymore. She kept to the open after that her back, mostly out of her beloved sunlight, except for all the times Grandfather, or Rain, or Red Cloud had patiently lifted her and taken her into the camp where she could feel the sun. She wondered how many weeks, how many months they had been lifting her and carrying her, and how they must have hated it.

Jane Ann had not remembered to bring water with her and she was beginning to get thirsty. It would not be easy to get down off the horse and then get back up again, but she knew if she had to, she could do it. So she began to look for a stream or a creek. She had heard Grandfather talk about going to a creek where they fished, and Rain had mentioned a river being nearby. She remembered he said it was the Grande River, so it must be big and easy to spot. But she and the patient, plodding horse seemed to travel on for hours, and still she had not come to a stream or a river. Nevertheless, she continued to go the direction she thought was forward.

Jane Ann had been keeping her direction with the sun moving from her back to in front of her thinking this was taking her East when actually it was taking her West straight into Crow territory.

What she did not know was that a raiding party of Crow warriors had been trying for months to get near enough to Sitting Bull's camp to steal their horses. It was a harmless act of bravery that most young warriors practiced. It was special proof of a brave's honor and fearlessness if he could slip into his enemy's camp and steal his horses without being caught. It was an act somewhat like the act of touching another warrior with a coup stick, like the story about Red Cloud told to Jane Ann by Grandfather and Rena.

The little band of Crow braves had stopped and made camp just after crossing the big river. They were resting before the final few miles into the area where they expected to find the horses just waiting for them.

Jane Ann did not notice the smoke from the Crows' campfire. Before she realized what had happened, she found herself riding straight toward about 10 young Crow Indians, all painted in various shades of war paint. They were standing around packing their horses securely for the next few miles of their journey. One of them was putting out the campfire. They all stared unbelieving at the red-haired white girl riding astride a Sioux pony. One of them actually laughed and pointed at her, but she could not understand what he was saying in his native language.

She thought quickly about how to get out of the mess she had gotten herself into so stupidly. She tried to think of what Red Cloud, or Grandfather, or Rena, especially Rena, might say.

"Water," she said casually in Sioux, "I am looking for water." She pulled her horse to a halt. It seemed as if she stood there astride the pony for a long time before she got any further reaction. She wondered just for a moment if she had spoken Sioux correctly. Then she said it again as clearly as she could. Finally, she said it in English, "I am thirsty and I'd thank you to tell me where water is, please."

At that, the whole Crow party howled and laughed. No one could have felt more silly than Jane Ann at that moment. She wondered if her whole life was going to be filled with silly or stupid moments like this. In desperation, she laughed with them.

The one putting out the fire stood up and came toward her. He grabbed her by a handful of red hair and pulled her from the horse. Jane Ann landed in a painful heap at his feet. The horse moved away. She knew then she was in trouble. Then she realized they may not be Sioux! They just might be as friendly as the young Sioux hunters who had dug her out of the snow and saved her life. Or they just might not be friendly at all.

As she was being dragged around by her hair, she realized her wounded ankle was being banged about even more. Oddly it did not hurt like she thought it would. Maybe it was all healed anyway. She could recognize the catcalls and sarcastic things they must be saying as they made fun of her. Then, she came to a stop and he let go her hair.

She tried to sit up but she was dizzy from being pulled around in circles. Someone else grabbed her hair and this time she felt a knife as he cut off a handful of her thick red curls. Another one of them kicked her and spit on the ground beside where she was. The one who cut off her curls tied them together quickly and then tied them to his own head. It looked like he had half her hair in his, so she figured she must be half-bald by then. Finally they must have tired making fun of her and all of them walked away.

Jane Ann hoped they had finished their fun and they would just get on their horses and ride away. She was hoping her own horse stayed where it was because she would hate to be alone without a way to get around someplace. But where and which direction she did not know.

"Oh, dear God," Jane Ann thought, "If only I had someplace to go, if only I knew how to get to anyplace!" She spit out a mouthful of dirt and she heard one of the Crow laugh.

"English," she heard him say with contempt. Then he hit her on the back and said a lot of words in his language, and then again he repeated, "English!"

Before he could hit her again, Jane Ann screamed, "English, yes!"

They all laughed and pointed and then the one that spat on the ground started toward her. For some reason she did not want him near her, and something in his eyes made her so afraid!

"Sioux dog," the Crow said, and he spit again very near where Jane Ann was.

She looked him straight in the eye and pulling herself up as tall as she could sit, she screamed firmly, "No, no, English, I am English."

He put his hand over his mouth and laughed like she had said something very funny. He turned to the others then and talked for a few minutes. They all got on their horses, including the one with her curls pinned in his own hair, and they turned and rode away in the direction from which she had just come.

Then the man with the angry eyes came over and lifted her to her feet. At that moment she realized she had lost her walking stick. There would be no way for her to stand up unless she held onto him. So, she held on to the warrior with all her might. He tried to shake her off, to push her away, but she held on and held on. Finally, he threw her to the ground and walked away, sounding like he was cursing under his breath.

He whistled and his horse came to where he was standing. He mounted and turned to yell something to her she did not understand, then he motioned for her to get up on the horse with him.

He did not know she could not stand because of her broken ankle. However, as she leaned where he threw her down, her long skirt had pulled up to reveal the large red slash that ran down her leg, and the carefully placed arrangement of animal skins and wooden rods which had been meant to protect her ankle. Now some of them were broken, some even were sticking into her skin causing her painful ankle to bleed again.

He stood there astride his horse looking at the helpless red-haired English girl, dressed like a Sioux woman. He wondered for a minute who she was and where she had come from, and more important, why she was there. It could be a trick by the Sioux to trap them. The Sioux may have known they were coming and sent her out for a decoy.

Maybe even at this very moment, his fellow Crow braves were on their way to being slaughtered by the Sioux. He dug his heels in his horse's side and the horse reared. he tried to make the horse's feet land on the woman, but they missed. He tried several times more and failed. Finally, he turned his horse in disgust, and scattering her pony from the clearing, he rode off to join the others.

As the angry brave was leaving, he suddenly changed his mind. Without warning, he jumped off his horse and lifted the girl up and placed her on the horse, and jumped up behind her.

Jane Ann was not sure what the brave intended on doing but at least she was still alive. She closed her eyes and thanked God for her life. At that moment, White Buffalo Woman appeared and, touching Jane Ann lightly on her face, she seemed to smile. Jane Ann could hear her say, "Believe, all will be well." Then Jane Ann had to hold on for dear life. She was being bounced up and down as the horse ran over rough ground, with the wind blowing her hair this way and that.

As they came into the camp, people who were busy doing their daily chores stopped and looked up at Black Sky riding fast into the middle of the camp, with someone held tight in front of him. He rode across to his own tipi and yodeled his arrival to someone inside. A woman opened the tipi flap and stepped out. It was an older woman with stone gray hair and a toothless smile. Black Sky announced something to her that Jane Ann did not understand except the word "Sioux", and then without warning, he lifted her and threw her to the ground. On landing, her head hit hard and she knew she would get a terrible headache from this!

As soon as she woke later, she knew the blow had knocked her unconscious. Her head did hurt. She was in a dark place, she supposed inside a tipi. She waited for her vision to clear but it did not. Then she realized she was bound hand and foot! Her eyes were bound also so that she could not see. Her ankle was on fire and she wondered in her heart, "Dear God, how can I get out of here?" She was so thirty! Yet, there was a smell so terrible it made her want to retch!

All the activity seemed to be outside. There were shouts and screams and guns going off outside. But there was also laughing and talking like there usually was at a celebration. She could hardly believe they would be celebrating the capture of one English girl. Finally she heard movement nearby inside the tipi or wherever she was.

"Sh.h.h!" a woman's voice whispered. "Do not make a sound, not a sound." The voice was so low that Jane Ann could hardly make out what she was saying.

Hands loosened the band around her eyes and it fell away. She was relieved to see someone was helping her. Then her hands were untied. She sat up and finished untying her legs. Her ankle hurt so bad! At least, as long as it was hurting, she knew she still had an ankle!

Jane Ann expected to see the toothless old woman whom she saw last as she fell from the horse to the ground the day before. But not so. The girl that was helping her was very young, possibly around her own age, fifteen or sixteen. She was dirty and her hair looked as if it had not been brushed in a long time. She had marks and bruises on her face and almost everywhere that was not covered. She couldn't be sure if they were bruises or dirt.

Jane Ann tried to motion that she was thirsty and needed water. The girl seemed terrified that Jane Ann was going to make a sound. Her eyes were wide and she was shaking her head vigorously for Jane NOT to speak.

"Crawl!" the girl motioned with her hands. Then like a rabbit, the girl crawled under the edge of the place they were and then was gone.

Jane Ann followed without knowing where she was heading. At least she would be going away from danger that she knew about. Suddenly she realized her head was splitting. She hoped she would not have to stop for any reason, that she could keep her head clear and escape this awful place!

Jane Ann followed as well as she could, crawling after the girl, under the edge of the tent or tipi and into the darkness. She gave herself a second to clear her eyes and then continued to crawl as best as she could see to follow the girl. She finally found her sitting with her back to a tree. She pulled herself over and sat beside her.

Jane Ann looked at the girl for a moment and wondered who she was and why she was there. She supposed the girl must be wondering the same about her. She started to speak but the girl put her hand over Jane Ann's mouth. She could see in the dark the girl was shaking her head. This meant, Jane Ann reckoned, that she should not speak at all.

Both women rested, Jane Ann wondering which direction to head first. After all, the girl had two good legs and feet with which to run if she had to, while Jane Ann was stuck with crawling around. Oh, how Jane wished she had the walking stick Red Cloud had given her!

At the thought of Red Cloud, tears welled up in Jane Ann's eyes, and a terrible pain filled her chest. To think that she would never see Red Cloud again, ... or Rena . . . . or Grandfather . . . . or any of her Sioux friends . . . . and maybe never to see Uncle Percy or Aunt Agnes again. The tears flowed freely from her eyes as she resisted with all her might making even the tiniest of sounds.

Minutes more passed, then the girl motioned to Jane Ann to follow her. The girl stood up and moved silently into the night leaving Jane Ann helpless leaning against the tree. When Jane Ann did not follow her, the girl turned around *AND* came back motioning again for Jane Ann to come, follow her. Jane Ann pointed to her ankle and, not wanting to make a sound, she put her hands together and apart like crushing something. She hoped the girl would understand she was meaning to let her know she had crushed bones in that ankle. The girl kept motioning her to follow.

Like a shadow out of the darkness, a hand suddenly came up holding a knife and with a few downward slashes, the girl gasped and slid to the ground.

Jane Ann crawled and scooted across the ground over to the girl and found she was still breathing. The man who had done this chuckled in the darkness. What a sight she must have made crawling over the ground like an animal! It took a real animal to stand and watch two helpless girls hiding in terror. Jane Ann then pulled herself up and leaned over the motionless girl. She was still alive! If the arm slashed out with the knife again, maybe, Jane Ann thought she could shield the girl from any further blows. She tensed her body and waited for the feel of the blade.

The man reached down and grabbed Jane Ann and hauled her over his shoulder. He then proceeded to walk with her into the camp, all the time Jane Ann was beating his back and screaming to be let go. When they came into the light of the fire, Jane Ann was shocked to see that the man was wearing an American Cavalry uniform. As he patted her on the bottom unceremoniously, he was whispering, "You ain't much now, girl, but old Sheffield has got you now and we're going to improve on that, you'll see!"

CHAPTER 12

The Crow Indian called Black Sky came up from his squat like a banshee surprised by an enemy. He was screaming and he looked like he was aching to fight the white man, Sheffield, who was carrying Jane Ann over his shoulder.

"Ah, wait a while there, bub," the man spit a big wad of tobacco out at Black Sky's feet, "Yer ain't going to fight nobody." He laughed again and he spit again. "I got everything yer need and yer knows it!"

Jane Ann was hitting Sheffield as hard as she could on his back with her fists. "Let me down!" Jane Ann was screaming as loud as she could.

Finally, Sheffield must have felt he had the Crow braves under control, so he heaved Jane Ann around and set her down hard. As soon as she hit solid ground, the pain burst through her ankle and leg so bad it caused her to lurch forward, and she fell sprawling over the brave who was sitting there closest to the fire. She pulled back and as she did, her elbow hit him full on the nose and he yelped and threw her away from him. This gave Black Sky a chance to get to her and he did. Whatever he was yelling to Sheffield made him madder than ever, and Sheffield suddenly lifted his hand revealing the long knife he was holding. With several swift slashes, he had totally stopped Black Sky who then fell bleeding across the struggling form of Jane Ann.

The toothless woman Jane Ann had seen the day before now came running out to where Black Sky lay unmoving. Jane Ann guessed this must be the man's mother. She was screaming and crying and trying to get Black Sky to get up.

Then the Crow brave who still had her long curls tied to his hair grabbed Jane Ann and pulled her out from under Black Sky's bleeding body, across and away from the fire. As the brave lifted her, she could hear a gurgling sound coming from Black Sky and his mother screaming even louder.

The Crow braves were yelling and screaming and running around by now as if they didn't know what to do. Finally, the one holding Jane Ann, barked a few orders and those who were beating the man, Sheffield, stood back so he could get up. Others started helping Black Sky's mother get him out of the middle of everything. The whole area started clearing out. From where she was being held, Jane Ann could smell a strong odor of whiskey, something much stronger than the whiskey her Uncle Percy kept in with his supply of medicines. And also much stronger than that in Papa's liquor cabinet. This whiskey smell was downright unpleasant. The Crow warrior that was holding her reeked of it!

He barked some more orders. To her surprise, Sheffield smiled and waved goodbye to her. She could see him still leering and cursing and laughing at her as the Indian carried her away toward a tipi.

Once inside, he put her down more gently than he had lifted her. She was grateful for that but she hoped he would leave soon! Instead, he sat down facing her. She thought he was looking at her but he was staring past her. She decided to stay still and bide her time, at least until she could try to get away again.

As if reading her thoughts, the man said to her in perfect Sioux, "I know who you are and why you came to Sioux country."

She suddenly could have scratched his eyes out. "Well, if you know so much, who are you and why are you pretending to be a Crow brave?" The look in her eyes could have melted metal.

He smiled without even flinching. "I know," he said, "That you are the English girl found by the young hunters. Your wounds were bad and Grandfather and Rena have been looking after you and tending your wounds. You were sent to warn the Sioux about the white man, so they would know what was going to happen and so they would be better prepared for it. Chief Sitting Bull and his nephew, Red Cloud, believe you were sent to us by White Buffalo Woman." He watched as what he was saying began to register in wonder on her face. "I am called Bear Claw, nephew of Sitting Bull and cousin of Red Cloud."

"What? What are you doing dressed and acting like a Crow warrior?" she paused and looked up at her red locks tied to his hair. "What are you doing pretending not to be who you are?" Her hand went up to her head where the hair had been unceremoniously snatched and cut. "Why did you cut my hair like that?" she whispered.

"I knew who you were the minute I saw you," he explained, "I was afraid you might remember me and say something that would get us both killed. I don't know why I chose to cut your hair like that. I'm sorry."

"Can you at least give me a drink of water?" she asked. "I'm so thirsty, I haven't had a drink of water in I don't know how long!"

"You could use a bath, too," Bear Claw said in a low voice, "too much Crow must not be good for you." He chuckled as he handed her a skin holding fresh spring water. "Besides, I should be asking you what you're doing out here in Crow territory. You should not be getting around with your ankle as bad as it is." He was pointing to the dried blood and broken cast that was suppose to protect it.

Jane Ann just nodded wearily. He was probably right on all points. Anyway, it was a relief to find out he was Sioux. She would not be as afraid of him now. Maybe he would protect her from the Crow. Maybe he would protect her from Sheffield. Then it suddenly dawned on her that if he was capable of cutting off a big chunk of her hair just to keep his role intact, what else would he do?

"Stay away from them all if you can," he warned her as if being able to know her thoughts. "I won't be able to stay with you all the time, but I can claim you now since Black Sky is dead."

"Claim me?" she asked while not believing what she was hearing.

"Yes, this is not pretend, this is real. I live with these people. I have to stand with them regardless of what happens to you. Listen, those people want to kill you. Right now, they think you are the cause of Black Sky being dead. He is their leader. They don't like having a dead leader. Believe me, they will kill you. Worse than them all is that white man, Sheffield. Never be alone with him! Never! He is known to use that knife in," and he paused and drew in a breath, "in crazy ways I couldn't even begin to explain. Just stay away from him!"

Then he walked over and pulled her to her feet while trying to hold her off her hurt ankle, "Yes, I claim you. According to those folks out there, you now belong to me and I can do anything I want with you. Nobody will care." Then he smiled at her. "Too bad you don't smell so good right now. I've had enough of that rotgut whiskey to do just about what I please. I'd rather do it with a clean girl with pretty hair though." He laughed out loud and let her down gently.

"Wait, at least you can go check on the girl that tried to help me." Jane Ann begged, "Sheffield slashed her with his knife and I tried to help her. She was bleeding pretty bad but she was still alive. Please go see if she still is, and help her."

He watched her for a minute, a smile at the corners of his lips. Something about his eyes reminded her of Red Cloud. She did not know if she could trust him or not. She did not have much choice.

Bear Claw left and was gone and then back in a very short time.

He shook his head. "That was Lillith, she was a miner's daughter and they were on their way West to California to the gold fields. A band of Crow killed her father and brought her here." He let that sink in. "She must have felt sorry for you."

Jane Ann shook her head, "Maybe she thought the two of us would have a better chance to get away."

"Forget her now," Bear Claw growled in a low voice, "You have to keep yourself alive. Say prayers if you want to but remember say some for yourself! This is going to be a rough ride!" He threw her a blanket and ducked down on his own at the other side of the tipi.

Jane Ann slept fitfully through the night not knowing what to expect from Bear Claw. If everyone got their names from what they did, maybe he got his from slashing out unexpectedly. That would sure fit what she had seen of him. He did exactly that when he cut her hair. Also, when he lugged her up off the ground. She finally gave up thinking about it. At least, she was alive. Then she remembered the crack Bear Claw had made about saying prayers. That wasn't such a bad idea! The least she could do for Lillith was pray that she was safely in the Spirit planes. And also to bless herself.

Just as daylight came, a woman lifted the flap to Bear Claw's tent and sat in a tin plate holding what looked like corn cakes. She placed a skin of water by it. She stared at Jane Ann sitting on one pallet and Bear Claw sleeping on another. Then she laughed as if she knew Jane Ann wasn't nearly good enough. She put her fingers up to hold her nose as if Jane Ann smelled bad. Then the girl left. It was taking awhile to sink in, but Jane Ann was beginning to agree with them all about the bad smell. She wondered what was in that tipi or whatever that place was where they had her tied up and blindfolded.

Jane Ann called Bear Claw, then she shushed calling his name. What if that was his Sioux name but not what the Crow called him! She could get them both killed. Well, that was one little important thing he forgot to tell her, what they called him! She wondered as she looked at him waking up what other important little fact he had left out.

"Wake up," she growled. "Your lady friend brought your food to you."

"Oh, you have got to go bathe and get that stench washed off!" He turned over and, for a minute, she thought he was going to go outside. Then he turned around, "Alright, listen carefully I'm only going to talk to you once. Get yourself ready, I'm going to lift you and the blanket and take you to the creek where you can wash up." He was putting soap and a clean blanket and some of his own clothes in a leather bag. "You are going to have to put these on after you wash." Then, "Yeah, be sure to get the blanket clean."

Without anymore warning, he scooped her and the blanket and the bag up and off they went out and across by the next tipi to the clearing leading to the creek. Once there, he sat her down and told her to take her clothes off. He began taking his off. Then he lifted her, naked as a baby, and walked into the creek. He held and pulled her until they got under a waterfall and then he let her go gently.

"Sorry," he said, "We have an audience out there." Then he remembered, "Jane Ann, I'm sorry about your ankle. I know this hurts, but it has to be washed clean anyway. They had you tied up in the death house, the place they store the dead bodies of enemies. The Crow don't put their enemies up on funeral biers like the Sioux, they burn them, and sometimes they store a lot of bodies first and then burn them all at once."

Jane Ann felt as if she was going to faint. To think of being tied up in the middle of a tipi full of rotting dead bodies was the limit in twisted horror.

"But you are alive, Jane Ann," Bear Claw whispered, "Alive, girl, and you've got to stay that way!"

Jane Ann stared at him. She did not know quite what to think of him. He surely was not like Red Cloud at all. But, maybe they were more alike than Jane Ann could guess. After all, she remembered, Red Cloud had walked out on her without a word back at the Sioux camp. Without a word! At least, Bear Claw talks a lot. So Jane Ann scrubbed and scrubbed. As she washed her hair, she took another good look at him and wished with all her might that those locks of hers that he had tied to his own hair would get loose and float away!

He took the soap and began to wash her back. She felt his hands moving slowly and she wondered what he was thinking. She remembered what he had said the night before. She also remembered her Mama telling her about becoming a woman. All that she remembered did not make the sensation of his hands on her naked back disappear. Long after their bath together, she would be looking at him and wondering about those hands on her back.

Right then though she asked him, "What name do you go by to the Crow?"

He laughed out loud. "He Who Walks Alone, that's my Crow name." He laughed again and Jane Ann wondered what was so funny. "You can call me Bear Claw though."

Back at the tipi, he called their medicine man, Crazy Dog, in to look at Jane Ann's ankle. He prodded and peered while Jane Ann did her best not to cry out in pain. She couldn't tell what the medicine man was saying to Bear Claw and she didn't much care. She just wanted him to stop poking at her hurt ankle. Finally, he left.

"Oh, I did not think I could stand any more of that!" Jane Ann breathed.

"Well, stay alert, he's coming back with his medicine bundle and some sticks. I doubt he will do as good a job as Grandfather." He was handing her some cakes and the water skin. "Eat, you will need it." We have to fix our next meal. I doubt my girl will do it since you are going to be here." He gave her a wink.

To pass the time, over the next few days, and to keep her close by him in an effort to keep her safe, he began to teach her the Crow language. Jane Ann had been happy just to learn the Sioux language. If she learned the Crow, too, then she ought to be able to travel around anywhere in the west in safety. To which, Bear Claw just laughed.

"You could not be safe no matter where you go," he teased her, "You attract danger to you. For example, do you know the cavalry man, Sheffield, wants to give the Crow a hundred guns and a pardon from jail if any one of them is ever caught by the Cavalry doing anything illegal?"

"What would he offer them that for?" she asked wondering if he was teasing her.

"For you, my girl." Then he suddenly reached across and kissed her full on the lips. "Remember, I said you are mine to do with as I please."

Jane Ann was trying to breathe. He had kissed her! She had actually wanted him to kiss her! She must be crazy as a loon. She leaned across and kissed him back full on the lips.

Then they both heard Crazy Dog coming back to doctor her ankle.

"It could wait," Jane Ann whispered to Bear Claw.

"Come back later," Bear Claw called to Crazy Dog. Too bad, though, but the medicine man was already in the tipi.

CHAPTER 13

By the time Crazy Dog had finished tending to Jane Ann's ankle, she realized what a mistake she had almost made. She was thankful he had returned as quickly as he did. By the time he was finished, she was looking at Bear Claw differently than before. She had time to think clearly, and she was positively sure that she didn't want to become close physically with someone she hardly knew.

Bear Claw had also thought over their situation. It would not be right to take advantage of a woman as young and inexperienced as Jane Ann was. Already he had ruined her beautiful head of hair by impulsively cutting it and attaching it to his own. Now that she was in his web, helpless as his prisoner, he felt uneasy about taking advantage of her. They hardly knew each other.

He had watched closely as Crazy Dog tended her crushed and broken ankle, twice broken in places that should have begun to heal already. He had seen her endure over an hour of lifting, moving, placing bone chips without any show of pain but an occasional sigh and the pallor that had set in when some stitches had to be done. She needed to be back among friends who would tend her wounds carefully and ensure that she receive the rest and good food that she needed to get back on her feet.

When Crazy Dog left, Bear Claw lifted Jane Ann gently and put her on her sleeping mat. She did not fuss or complain. She did not tease him about what she would or would not do or about what he could or could not do to her. Her energy had been spent enduring the pain of tending her ankle. She was weak and pale. As he lifted her he felt her whole body trembling like a leaf being blown by the wind.

He watched her as she went to sleep. While he was watching her, he looked at how big his shirt and pants were on her tiny frame. She had tied the waist with a rope. Although he had a small waist, hers was much smaller. She had rolled the pants legs up several times so as not to trip when she stood. Somehow, sleeping like she was, she looked tiny and helpless. He took another blanket and covered her securely. Then he realized he did not want to take his eyes off her. But, instead, he crawled in his sleeping mat and made himself shut his eyes anyway.

Outside he could hear Sheffield drunkenly calling, "Little Jane Ann," in English so only she would understand. "Come and lay with your beloved."

That's when Bear Claw knew he was going to have to shut up that drunken fool before the night was over. Soon though the whiny voice stopped. Then it seemed that the whole camp went to sleep. There was peaceful silence. Not even a camp dog whined or barked. Just wonderful quiet, and Bear Claw went to sleep.

The next morning, neither one discussed the events of the day before. When they had finished eating their morning meal, Bear Claw knew that he must go with the others on their raid that day, or else someone would question why. He could not pretend to sleep with his woman all day every day from then on. Yet, he was very concerned with how Jane Ann would be treated while he was away. It was critical that she stay off that ankle now until it had started to mend a little.

Once he was gone, he knew how the Crow women would act, especially Dark Sky's mother. He had already seen evidence of their treatment of strangers with the girl, Lillith. The girl had been beaten, spit on, cursed, and not allowed to eat food in peace or drink water or even bathe. She was made to eat what little she had in the death house.

Jane Ann needed a walking stick to help her get around. She also needed a weapon with which to defend herself. If he were out with the Crow, and Sheffield slipped off and came back for Jane Ann, Bear Claw wanted her to have a way to defend herself.

When he talked to Jane Ann, she shook her head. "I don't know. Bear Claw," she had told him, "I remember trying to learn how to shoot a gun when Papa was alive, and neither of us had much luck with it."

"Then I won't go with them," said Bear Claw. "I will insist I have to stay here with you."

When some of the Crow came to call him from his tipi to go hunting, he refused in an angry voice. He yelled for them to "Get away, dogs."

Even though Jane Ann did not know what he was saying in Crow language, she understood the tone of his voice.

For a few days longer, his angry voice fooled them into allowing him to remain with Jane Ann. Then they became insistent. They even came and told him that the Sioux were coming to their village to steal Jane Ann back and steal their horses at the same time.

Bear Claw refused to answer them.

Finally, on another day, a large group of Crow came. This time, Sheffield came with them. They announced that Sheffield had bought and paid for the girl, and that it was time now for Bear Claw to hand her over. He had her long enough. They wanted him to give her to Sheffield that day.

Bear Claw was hoping the Crow who told him the Sioux were coming the day before was right, and that they were on their way. If so, they would arrive soon. But now, with Sheffield "buying" Jane Ann, perhaps they would not come soon enough.

"Get away from my tipi," he shouted to the Crow. Then, in a moonstruck voice, he called pleading, "Haven't you ever had a woman you could not let go for awhile? Then after the fire cools down, you can then leave and stay away a long time?"

Jane Ann's eyes grew wide even though she had not understood all of what he said, and she blushed.

Sheffield kicked at the tent flap. "Open up, you liar, you're just a coward trying to buy time because you are afraid to fight anymore." His voice whined no matter what he was saying. "Come on out, little baby, and we will hold your hand."

Bear Claw tensed up his fists. He wanted to go out and beat the daylights out of that big coward. Instead, he stayed where he was. This was a nasty little game and the first one to crack lost. He had seen it played too many times with Sheffield.

"Get on and leave me alone," Bear Claw warned, "And while you are out today, do your best to get your head blown off, Sheffield, I can't think of anyone who deserves it more."

Outside, curses and more curses. The Crow braves finally talked Sheffield into leaving them alone. They practically dragged him off kicking while promising another bottle of whiskey. Bear Claw hoped they all got drunk.

He did not leave the tipi anymore after that incident. It would be too easy for Sheffield to be waiting and no telling what he would do to Jane Ann. Or where he would take her.

Jane Ann knew they could not stay inside the tipi forever. They had to get out and leave, but she would hold them up no matter where they were heading or what time they tried to go. She thought if only she could walk or run, if only she had not lost the walking stick Red Cloud had given her. If only she had not run away!

Papa had always said that only a real coward runs away. Jane Ann wondered why she was remembering that just now, and why she had not thought of that before she slipped out of the Sioux camp like a rat in the middle of the night.

When her head started hurting again, she looked for White Buffalo Woman, for her Mama or Grandmother Rogers, for her mother, Dorothy, for anyone who would help her and tell her what to do, or what was going to happen. She wondered if they had forsaken her.

"Bear Claw," Jane Ann said softly, "If I should begin to talk strangely to you, please help me to remember what I say. I have a terrible headache. Usually such a headache means White Buffalo Woman wants to tell me about something that is going to happen or that is happening now. Will you let me talk and help me remember?"

"Of course," Bear Claw agreed. He had not realized she was a medicine woman. Of course, he would watch and listen. He would remember.

Deep in the middle of the night, he heard Jane Ann stir. Then she moaned. She was very restless and he thought it might be the pain of her head or her ankle. But she settled down until early just before daybreak.

Jane Ann touched Bear Claw lightly on the arm. "Help me, Bear Claw, please help me remember what I say. White Buffalo Woman is here."

He got up immediately and moved closer to Jane Ann. He watched as a glow appeared to shine around her face. She looked ecstatic as if she was seeing a Spirit. She began talking in English and he did not understand every word she was saying. Soon though she changed to Sioux and in a low voice she whispered that "Everything is going to be alright. You are going to be set free and go home." That was all he understood, and he wondered who it was that was going to be set free and go home. White Buffalo Woman could have been talking to either one of them or maybe to both. He hoped it was to both. He was fast losing hope on being able to keep the stand-off going. His only ace in the hole was Crazy Dog and he was hoping that old coot was going around telling everybody about their loving kiss.

The next morning was a repeat of the same thing they had put up with all week. A band of Crow braves wanted to go down into Shoshone territory and bring back some horses. Sheffield helped them plan the whole raid, they said. They wanted Bear Claw to go along since he knew the trail better than any of them. Instead of arguing and refusing to go, Bear Claw agreed to come with them.

Jane Ann nodded. She thought she would be fine. He had gathered in enough for her to eat already so that she would not have to go outside the tipi. She would stay inside until he returned.

"Stay away from the Crow women," Bear Claw warned her again. "Especially Dark Sky's mother," he had already told her these things, "She is pretty mean and she holds a grudge."

"Go on and come back soon. Thank you for taking care of me." She kept assuring him she would be alright.

Bear Claw had refused the Crow renegades and Sheffield all week and she had grown accustomed to the haggling between he and the braves every morning. Now, though, she could understand that he thought he had dragged it out long enough. Somehow she knew she would be alright. At least, she tried to believe it, and she tried to convince him she believed it.

He left her with a long knife. He warned her if anyone but Crazy Dog came into the tent, to use it. Then he warned her that Sheffield might slip away and come back here for her. If he did, she was to get away from him anyway she could. Jane Ann nodded but she already knew that man's strength, and she knew that she would have little time to do anything other than use the knife. She had never hurt anyone before. Maybe it would not come to that.

She heard the raiding party ride out in the dark of early morning. She did not sleep but stayed as still as possible hoping everyone would forget that she was in Bear Claw's tipi.

As the sun rose, someone came to the tipi entrance and coughed. "Good morning, girl with red hair," the voice of Crazy Dog said.

"Good morning," Jane Ann answered him.

"I wish to look at your bandage again, just to make sure it is staying on. You let me come in?" he asked her very quietly as if he did not want anyone to hear him.

"Yes, come in," she said as she made sure she had the knife in her hand under the blanket.

He brought a kettle of steaming tea and two corn cakes. He set them beside her and motioned for her to eat. At first, she thought it might be a trick and she shook her head. He settled himself down at the foot of her sleeping mat where he could get a look at her bandages. He took some strange looking metal cage out of his bag.

"I put this together myself," Crazy Dog explained, "Your leg is never going to heal up as long as you keep getting it hurt. With this metal cage around it, your leg will be protected. It will help you get around better. You will be able to put your weight on it with the use of a walking stick."

It sounded like a pretty good idea to Jane Ann. He set to work doing the best he could to strengthen her bandages. He worked slow but steady, stopping only to listen to voices talking outside, and to notice Jane Ann had relaxed and was enjoying the tea and corn cakes.

After he was satisfied with the sturdy construction of the cage around her leg, sure that it would not come off easily, he helped her to stand and test it out. From behind him, he brought forward her walking stick, the one Red Cloud had given her! She could not believe her eyes.

"How did you know?" Jane Ann asked him. "Where did you find it?" She took it eagerly and caressed the wood. She thought she had lost it for good, and here it was in her hands again!

"Bear Claw told me it came off when you were pulled off your horse on the other side of the river." He kept glancing back at the entrance, "back in the clearing where you first struggled with him, Dark Sky and the others.

I went to look for it and sure enough there it was." He smiled broadly, obviously very pleased with himself.

He was still talking very low as if he did not want anyone to hear them. Maybe he knew something was going to happen any minute. She had an uneasy feeling, too, like the feeling she had after White Buffalo Woman warned her and her family about the avalanche and they went ahead anyway. This was the same kind of feeling, like something was going to happen no matter what was done to prevent it, no matter how much warning. But that everything was going to turn out alright though in the end.

It was about noon, Jane Ann guessed, because she could hear the women stirring around their pots getting food ready to eat. The children were running back and forth playing their games. Occasionally, she could hear humming as she had in the Sioux camp but not as often. She told Crazy Dog to go on when he wanted to and get something to eat, but he just shook his head. She offered him some berries that Bear Claw had left for her. He accepted a handful.

Just as she swallowed her berries, the entrance flap to the tipi was suddenly thrown back. She could smell him even before he entered uninvited. That pungent smell of bad whiskey that he reeked of, it was Sheffield! Just as Bear Claw had warned, Sheffield had come to get her!

She leaned down to reach under the blanket for the knife and her hand just found it when Sheffield lunged toward her with tobacco dripping from the corners of his mouth. He hit her hard as he landed against her, and it knocked the breath out of her for a minute. She was afraid she would lose the knife under the blanket but so far she had not. She held to it tight while he tried to catch her under her chin and turn her head around.

Then she heard a hard thud. Air came out of Sheffield's mouth in a long rush. She could feel it on the left side of her face back of her ear. He slid down across her legs. Jane Ann looked down at him in her lap. She saw a glazed look slowly cover his eyes. It took her a little while to realize Sheffield was dead. How? She had not even used the knife!

Then she looked up and saw Crazy Dog smiling. "Dumb white eyes jackass," Crazy Dog mumbled as he pulled the dead man off her legs. "We are pretty smart fixing your leg like that. Look how good the cage works! You didn't get your leg hurt any- again just before he dragged Sheffield outside the tipi. "That Bear Claw is pretty smart alright. He told me how to fix the cage. He made me promise to go get the stick. He sent me to stay here with you until he comes back. Pretty smart, huh!" He was still smiling as he hauled Sheffield off to the death house. He left the flap open and Jane Ann started shivering, but not from the cold air. She was shivering from fear! It was all over and she was still scared! She tried hard to calm down.

Later, the woman looked inside the tent. It was the same girl that had brought food for Bear Claw the first day. She didn't come in but she was curious. She looked carefully at Jane Ann and then walked away.

"Well, maybe she was just looking for Bear Claw, or Crazy Dog," Jane Ann reasoned. But she had begun to shiver like she was freezing to death! She wished the woman had not stared at her like that.

Then she heard Crazy Dog arguing with someone. He hurried up and came over to stand at the entrance to the tipi. After he looked in and made sure Jane Ann was still alright, he started yelling at someone. Jane Ann calmed down enough to listen and figure out he was telling somebody off, sending them away from there. After he was satisfied they had left, he came in the tent and shut the flap down.

"Long day," Crazy Dog muttered. "Lots of crazy jackasses." He nodded to her and then watched her a minute. "You alright now. Jackasses gone, they're not brave at all. I won't leave you. I promised Bear Claw. You rest now."

Jane Ann was real glad when she finally stopped shivering. She was glad Crazy Dog was with her, too.

After awhile, Jane Ann remembered that she had Bear Claw's clothes on. She felt embarrassed, and she wondered what Crazy Dog thought. She wondered where her own clothes were, and then she remembered how bad she and the clothes had smelled. Bear Claw had made her wash the blanket (with his help!) but she didn't remember being told to wash her clothes. Maybe he threw them away. That meant she would just have to keep wearing Bear Claw's pants and shirt. She couldn't even find her own jacket only an old one of Bear Claw's and, even if it swallowed her in size, it was just right to keep her warm.

The afternoon passed by with the two of them inside the tipi. Crazy Dog was funny. He would doze awhile, and then suddenly he would get up and move something out of the way, or stoke the fire, or something. He looked as if he were doing what Aunt Agnes back in London had called "busy work." when Tillie would busy herself moving things around in a clean room, or else polish something again that she'd already polished. Tillie had been trying to look busy. Now here was Crazy Dog doing the same.

Jane Ann offered Crazy Dog an out. "You can go while I take a nap," she told him, but he refused to leave her. Then he sat back down. It looked like he did not intend to leave her until Bear Claw returned. She was glad for that.

Then Crazy Dog took out a deck of cards. The raiding party had not returned yet and Crazy Dog had to do something, so he began to show Jane Ann some magic tricks he had learned from the "white eyes" soldiers. It seemed like he did the card tricks for a long time. Jane Ann's eyes could hardly stay open when he finished.

"It's good, the day is over. You sleep. I keep watch." Crazy Dog motioned her to go to sleep. She wished she wasn't so tired. All that shaking and being scared earlier in the day had exhausted her. If it had not been for Crazy Dog's card tricks and occasional talking, she thought she probably would have slept all day.

CHAPTER 14

That night, in the early morning hours, a Sioux raiding party rode in dragging behind their ponies burning sagebrush. They did not really intend to but sparks flew everywhere and burned the communal death house down along with several of the tipis. The Crow warriors who did not go with the raiding party to Shoshone territory put up a fight but they were no match for the Sioux warriors. After the battle was over and the Crow braves thought about it, they decided it had been Sitting Bull who attacked their camp. The way they told the story for years afterward, they didn't come out looking so bad. Indeed, to bravely fight Chief Sitting Bull, a mighty chief and skilled warrior, and come out alive was an honor in itself.

Crazy Dog didn't tell the story at all though. You'd have thought he was with the raiding party down getting Shoshone horses. After he killed Sheffield and put his body in the Crow death house, he went back and waited with Jane Ann. Somehow he suspected somebody was going to come for the girl. It had been over a week. Whoever was coming to get her was just waiting for the camp to be almost deserted. Sure enough, there were a dozen or so braves left behind, those who had drunk too much bad whiskey, some old folks, the women and children.

When the Sioux came riding in dragging their fire bushes, Jane Ann was asleep and Crazy Dog was dozing while sitting square in front of the entrance to the tipi. He was sitting there in case anybody came in, they would wake him up bumping into him in the dark. He smelled fire first, and then he heard the horses. The Sioux braves had covered and wrapped their horses' hooves but he had heard them anyway. He knew it was the Sioux and that they were coming after Jane Ann.

When the tipi flap was opened from the outside, Crazy Dog motioned to where Jane Ann was asleep, and then he nodded. Red Cloud nodded back at him. Crazy Dog was not about to make enemies with a Sioux, especially Red Cloud. He and Red Cloud's father were old friends. He knew Red Cloud when he was a little boy called Slow. Chuckling, Crazy Dog slipped out back into the woods until all the fires stopped.

Jane Ann woke up to the sounds of yelling and the smell of fire. She saw Crazy Dog in the shadows inside the tipi talking to somebody. Then he left. She started shivering and realized he was deserting her after all. She reached and found the knife. This time she was going to get it out from under the cover before the man got to her! So she could use it . . . she kept on saying to herself she could use it . . . . she intended to use it.

Then suddenly the tipi was on fire. Smelling the smoke, she turned her head away and started coughing. For awhile she did not see the man who lifted her up. When she did, her heart sang with joy. It was Red Cloud! With a steady gait, he brought Jane Ann, blanket and all, out to his horse and lifted her up. They had not spoken to each other. He squeezed her arm softly. He touched her hair where Bear Claw had cut a big hunk out of it. She was amazed that in the light of the burning camp he would take time to notice her hair. Then he jumped up behind her and yelled something to the others.

She recognized Rain and Left Hand and Right Hand. Jane Ann smiled. Not once, but twice she owed these men her life. "You will be taken home," White Buffalo Woman had told her earlier. "You will be safe." She was right again!

They rode for hours. She tried to stay awake but the steady gait of the horse and the warm feel of Red Cloud at her back made her keep dropping off to sleep. Somewhere deep inside, she thought of Bear Claw and wondered if she would ever see him again. She couldn't make sense of why on earth an English girl like herself would be here now riding all over the country at night with a Sioux Indian warrior. She felt like a very lucky person to have such high adventures.

They stopped to rest the other side of the river just about where Jane Ann had run into the Crow raiding party that day she ran away from

Sitting Bull's camp. She remembered how thirsty she had been that day. Now, here at the same place, were Red Cloud and Rain and the others bringing her water and food, anything she might need, without her even asking. She was staring at a log laying across the path where a fire had been built before wondering if it was the log she fell down by that afternoon, right before Bear Claw had cut the hunk out of her hair.

Red Cloud asked her if she wanted to get down and rest. She nodded. He helped her down off the horse and then, holding her steady, he reached over and pulled the walking stick out, handed it to her, and then turned and walked away. She thought it was amazing even that he had been able to see it in the early morning darkness in Bear Claw's tipi. She was glad he had though.

She watched him walk away from her. She wondered if they would ever be able to talk again. Perhaps she could never explain how she felt about her visions. Or how she felt about him . . . or about Bear Claw. Maybe he did not even care how she felt!

Rain walked over and greeted her. "Hi ho! Jane Ann, it is good to see you." In his usual friendly manner, he began to tell her how long they had been looking for her, how much Rena missed her. For perhaps the first time, she realized that Rain and maybe the rest of them really were her friends. Even more, she was beginning to feel they were her family. That brought her some measure of comfort. She wondered how in the world she could have run away from her family!

They rested awhile in the clearing. Rain took his horse over to the river where the others were standing. Jane Ann putting her foot gingerly on the ground, sighted a big rock and made her way over to it. She probably looked funny hobbling like that, jumping on her good foot, touching the ground lightly with the metal cage on her hurt foot. Yet she had to know whether it would work or not. And it did! She could get around by herself! She was grateful to Crazy Dog and Bear Claw for her new found ability to walk. It had been so long! No matter how funny she might appear, it was good to be upright again.

In the middle of her reverie, someone handed her a cup of water. She looked up and saw it was Red Cloud, without even a smile and no indication what he was thinking.

"Let's go now," was all Red Cloud said. He helped Jane Ann back on the horse. They all rode off and were soon back in Sitting Bull's camp by late afternoon.

As they rode in, everyone in the camp came running up to welcome her home. She could hear them saying, "Welcome home, Sioux Blessing Girl!" She began to look anxiously for Rena and Grandfather. What if those two dear ones who had saved her life did not want to see her now?

Sitting Bull was first to speak directly to her. "Coming home at last, our own Sioux Blessing Girl! Welcome!" Then, "We will have a celebration, a welcome celebration. Look! You can see our people are building a big fire, and preparing much good food to eat." He was beaming.

Jane Ann began to explain why she had run away, but he could not hear her with all the voices talking and yodeling and calling her name. Sitting Bull waved her on into the direction of Rena's tipi.

Red Cloud had already dismounted. He reached for Jane Ann's horse's reins and then he led her gently over to where Grandfather and Rena were waiting. They helped her from the horse. Rena hugged her and kept hugging her. Grandfather patted her hand and her shoulder and he kept saying how glad they were that she was back. "You are safe, now." He said over and over.

The tipi flap was up revealing a warm welcoming light inside from where the sun shone through the smoke hole overhead.

Jane Ann was amazed at her reaction to seeing them and the familiar tipi. It was coming home, and again she told herself she would never run away again. She wanted so to explain and tell them all why she had left and that she was wrong to run away like that. She wanted to say how happy she was to be back with them. Red Cloud, however, had simply vanished. He was nowhere to be seen.

On into the evening they sat with her, asking questions, then listening to her tell how she was ashamed of the visions she had been shown by White Buffalo Woman, that she just wanted to run away and hide because she was afraid they all would hate her for speaking aloud those visions.

"No, no!" Rena assured her, "We honor what White Buffalo Woman shows you and we are happy you trusted us with your visions. What you have is a BLESSING to you and to us. We were worried because of your ankle. We did not know where you were or how you got out and left. We were so afraid someone had come in and sneaked you away!" Rena hugged her again.

Jane Ann could see Grandfather staring at the cage around her leg. She smiled at him. "Grandfather," Jane Ann said, "look at what Crazy Dog has made for me." And she turned so he could get a good look at it. She pulled up the pants Bear Claw had let her wear to reveal to Grandfather the metal cage.

"Ah!" Grandfather exclaimed as he examined it very carefully. Then he saw the new bandage and where the blood was seeping through.

"Some of the bones were broken again," Jane Ann said softly, "Crazy Dog said you must be a miracle man to have set them so good before. He spent hours trying to get them in place again. Then yesterday, or the day before, I forget which, Crazy Dog came and put this cage on my foot. He said Bear Claw told him how to make it safe and strong so I can put my foot down and use the walking stick."

Grandfather nodded. He knew Crazy Dog a long time. For a Crow medicine man, he was a good man and a true healer. He was a friend and not an enemy. Medicine people do not have time to be enemies.

Rain came in then holding something behind his back. He had a wide grin on his face. Then Red Cloud came in next. The tipi was getting crowded!

Grandfather nodded for Rain to speak.

"Jane Ann, here is your paper to draw on with some paints and more charcoal from the Trading Post."

Jane Ann was delighted and surprised.

Rena pulled a hard-bound journal of writing paper from under the stack of blankets in the corner. "Here is what the trading post clerk said white people use for a journal to write in. Grandfather and I give you this with love."

Tears had begun to slip down Jane Ann's cheeks. It was like a birthday party! She did not want to cry at such a happy occasion.

Red Cloud leaned over and, without a word, he handed her a big book and some colored chalk which looked familiar to her. Then she realized it was hers from the wagon! Inside the book were drawings she had made on their ride from St. Louis. She looked at the sketches she had made of the group of Kickapoo Indians, at pictures of Mama and Papa. Now she was really crying and laughing at the same time.

"How can I tell you what this means to me?" She asked Red Cloud and then looked around at each of them. "You have brought something of my past back to me. These drawings are precious!" Then she wondered how she could ever have believed he did not care about her at all! None of them had been shunning her after the campfire revelations of White Buffalo Woman's visions. They had all been out looking for a way to let her know how much they appreciated them! As she thanked each one in turn, she told them how much this meant to her and she apologized for misunderstanding why they had left her. And for having run off and left them.

"Red Cloud," Jane Ann began, but then words failed her. She tried hard to clear her thoughts and to stop the tears from flowing down her cheeks. She tried to be calm and speak from her heart. "Red Cloud," she began again, but words failed her. "Red Cloud," she started again. Then she looked into his eyes and she saw his lips were trembling, and she felt his hands as they grabbed hold of her own, trembling like her own were. That's when she understood this man was her friend, too, her family, and she promised in her heart never to run away again. "Thank you, Red Cloud."

She thanked them each and in her heart promised each one she would never run away again. She could almost hear her Papa saying, "You've come of age, girl, it's about time!"

All those who loved her could not bear to ask about the Crow Indians who had taken her to their village. No one asked about her experiences as a prisoner of the Crow. What she didn't know was that Chief Sitting Bull had told them to wait until Jane Ann was sitting around his campfire that evening. Then they could all ask her questions. Not many women walked out of a Crow camp alive or in one piece. Sitting Bull figured it was important enough to talk about when the Council Elders were around. After all, they did not want her having to repeat the same descriptions over and over again. Once would be enough. That is why they all (Rena, Grandfather, Rain, Red Cloud, Left Hand and Right Hand) stayed close to her until it was time to go to Sitting Bull's campfire. However, it was Rena who suddenly noticed that Jane Ann was wearing men's clothes!

"Jane Ann, do you want to clean up and put on a dress before we go to celebration?" Rena asked as tactfully as possible.

Jane Ann nodded and whispered "Thank you!" She wanted to change into women's clothes, but still she dreaded not having Bear Claw's clothes on. She knew that would sound silly to anyone else, but wearing the clothes had made her feel brave.

Rena ran the men out of the tent. She hurried to get the new clothes she and Grandfather had made for Jane Ann. They were of the softest deerskin. Rena had sewed tiny birds and butterflies on the loose blouse with colored thread. She was proud of her work and how beautiful the dress looked on Jane Ann.

No one had said anything about her hair until Rena was helping her brush it. She saw right away the obvious big chunk that had been cut out by Bear Claw. Jane Ann did not tell Rena, or anyone else, that it was Bear Claw who did it. Rena brushed it and tried to hide it, but it was such a big chunk it was impossible to hide. The missing hair would be an obvious mark of her being a prisoner of the Crow peoples until it grew back. Nothing could change that. Some things cannot be changed right away.

It was time to go to the campfire by the time Jane Ann and Rena finished. As they came out of the tipi, Jane Ann noticed it was going to be a red sunset. The sky was bathed in a soft red glow like a light was going dim.

Grandfather noticed it, too. So did Red Cloud. They had been standing together watching the sky turn red as the women were inside dressing. Neither man spoke about it but both were remembering an old legend. When the sky turns red, there is going to be a big change in everything. Sometimes it's famine, sometimes drought, sometimes a war, but always it meant the people were going to have to move.

"See how well I can get around by myself." Jane Ann called, her words bouncing up and down like her whole self, bobbing up and down, as she came walking with the stick and the cage. They let her walk awhile.

Then Red Cloud reached and scooped her up in his arms and Rain grabbed the walking stick. "No need to get tired out on your first day home," Red Cloud said without smiling.

"Thank you again," Jane Ann whispered.

"No need." Red Cloud murmured in her ear.

The little group found their places around the communal fire. Everybody was talking and eating and drinking the warm tea Jane Ann had grown so fond of. It was a friendly, warm group of people here around the Sioux campfire, different from the other communal fire in the Crow camp where people argued and drank and cursed.

Rain had told her when they stopped at the clearing by the river, that the Crow Camp she was held prisoner in was a renegade camp, not one of the Crows' regular camps. Probably even the Crow peoples would be glad they had burned part of it down. She wondered after that conversation if Bear Claw was also a renegade. Perhaps that was why no one spoke about him at all.

After the social amenities were over, Chief Sitting Bull told Jane Ann they were all happy she had been rescued. He thanked Red Cloud, Rain, Left Hand, and Right Hand for being so brave and bringing Blessing Girl back to her Sioux peoples. He then asked if Jane Ann wanted to say anything.

"Yes," she said timidly. "I want to thank them also because they have saved my life not once but twice. I am grateful to you, my Friends!" Then she bowed her head to each one of her rescuers. Everyone in the camp agreed heartily and some hit their thighs, some hit the ground with sticks, other yodeled. It was a happy time for them all.

"Jane Ann," Chief Sitting Bull said, "You continue to be a blessing to us and each time you return to us there is something good that comes of it." He paused and looked around at the Council members. "This time, the soldiers have been called from Laramie and they are going back East to fight somewhere else. For now, the Sioux peoples will live in peace!"

Everyone cheered! Jane Ann felt humbled because she knew she had absolutely nothing to do with that happening, and she had not even been told about it by White Buffalo Woman. Yet it sounded like a good thing, especially when she remembered the man, Sheffield. Some day she would have to tell her friends about Sheffield. And about Bear Claw. For now, she just clapped her hands together and cheered like the rest of them.

CHAPTER 15

The water was ice cold on Jane Ann's feet. Yet, the sun shone warm in the sky. She had not been able to stay inside. She had been restless and she could not sit still to paint or work on her drawings. She had long since given up writing at length in her journal as she and George and Georgette promised they would do. What a childish thing to promise to meet again. This country was so vast and big, perhaps they would never see each other again. Perhaps she would never see Uncle Percy or Aunt Agnes again either. Those long ago years seemed exactly that now – they were long ago! She had her drawings and pictures she had drawn of each of them, and she cherished them. She had even brought them out and looked at them again that morning. Then she decided to go down to the creek to fish. To do what she was now doing, hanging her feet in the icy water.

Grandfather had said once that we are what our past experiences and associations have made us. There with her feet in the icy creek water, Jane Ann wondered about Bear Claw. What had made him a renegade? That is, if he, indeed, was one. Did knowing her change him? Did her knowing him change her? Lots of questions. What she was really wondering about was who was she?

Jane laughed bitterly. Why was she even thinking of Bear Claw? He knew where she was and he had never tried to see her. It had been over a year since Red Cloud, Rain and the others had rode in and rescued her. A long time since she had seen him. Why on earth would she keep remembering someone she'd seen fourteen days who had not contacted her in over a year? Instead she should be thinking about Red Cloud. He wanted her to be his second wife, to join him at his new camp where Sitting Bull had made him a Chief.

She had been thinking so hard she only had one fish to take back to Rena and Grandfather. She was one of the few people who could fish all afternoon and come home with only one fish. Knowing Rena, though, Jane Ann could already taste the fish stew she would prepare with one fish.

As she made her way back to camp, Jane Ann wondered if Grandfather was going to the trading post again anytime soon. They had closed it for awhile when the soldiers at the fort left. Now it was open again.

She heard horses behind her and she turned to see Red Cloud and some of the braves from his camp approaching. He waved to her and she waved back and stood waiting.

She could see he was not going to stop so she lay her fishing pole down and made sure the fish was secure in her big pocket, then she closed her eyes and waited to be lifted high onto his horse. Sure enough, he leaned down and scooped her up without any hesitation. The horse was still galloping toward camp. The others with him yodeled admiration.

"You smell like fish," he teased her when he put her down in front of her tipi. His hand still rested on her shoulder. "When will you be my wife, Jane Ann?" he asked still holding her shoulder lightly. He was leaning down making her look him straight in the eyes.

"Today," she teased, "Maybe today you want to marry a fish wife and everybody will say, 'Look at Red Cloud who married a smelly fish wife, look at her limp across the camp.'"

Red Cloud let go her shoulder and straightened up with a frown on his face. "Go, talk to Rena, get in a better mood before I see you next." He turned his horse and rode off toward Sitting Bull's tipi.

She didn't know why she had spoken so sullenly to Red Cloud. He had every right to expect she would let him know soon. He had been asking her to marry him for three years! She knew she cared for him. She should be deliriously happy. He was one of the kindest people she had ever known. She tried to shake off her self-pitying feelings. Jane Ann turned finally and went into her tipi.

She gave her lonely fish to Rena who was happy to add it to the day's stew.

"You can ask Red Cloud to join us for supper, Jane Ann." Rena said.

Jane Ann didn't really hear her. She was already pulling out her drawing paper and had her mind on something else. "Rena," Jane Ann decided suddenly, "I'm going back to the creek to just sit and draw for awhile. Is that alright with you?"

"Yes, but come back for supper, please, Jane Ann," Rena watched her put her drawing supplies in a bag and throw it over her shoulder. "She is restless," Rena thought and she wondered why.

Jane Ann sat for hours, until the sun began setting and dark shadows played across the sky. She looked at her drawing and smiled. It was a good likeness even to the red curls tied in the man's hair. She would give anything to see him right now. It would help in her decision whether to become Red Cloud's second wife or not.

Later, when she came back for supper, Red Cloud was there waiting for her. They all ate and then Rena and Grandfather politely left them sitting alone around the fire.

"Have you an answer for me this evening?" Red Cloud asked Jane Ann.

"Yes, I do have an answer. Perhaps not the one you want right now but please be patient with me." She peered at him under her lashes. "I have to tell you something first and you may not like it." She paused again wondering where to start, how much to say about Bear Claw.

While she was thinking about what to say, Rain came running. "Red Cloud, hurry, the trading post is on fire and Sitting Bull wants us to take water to help the white man! Hurry!"

"You've been saved again from opening your honest heart to me, Jane Ann," Red Cloud said while rising to his feet. He pulled her up, too, and stood there holding her hands in his for a moment. "When I return, we will talk, but be ready to say yes or no." "I don't need long explanations or reasons for your decision. Just YES or NO. Do you understand me?" He held under her chin lightly so she had to look up into his eyes. He thought he could see tears in hers, but he was not sure in the light of the campfire.

While the men were all out of the camp helping the white man fight the fire at the Trading Post, a rider came into camp looking for Chief Sitting Bull. Because he had gone with the others to fight the fire, the man asked then to speak to the medicine man.

When Jane Ann heard that they had a visitor from the Crow camp across the river, she ran out to see who it was. Grandfather had already started toward the visitor, and he and Jane Ann hurried to catch up so they walked together.

"Why are you so anxious to see a Crow?" he asked her, amused that she was so eager to see a stranger that she would run out and greet them. It was not like her at all.

"It might be Bear Claw," Jane Ann answered, "Or Crazy Dog."

Grandfather laughed. She certainly had a long memory. That, he knew already from her drawings, one of them of Crazy Dog, that she had memories she had shared with no one. He had looked at the picture she had drawn of Crazy Dog. He had been proud to look at his old friend once again, and honored that she would show him, headdress and all, looking like he was presiding over a great healing of some kind. Funny though that she had never mentioned Bear Claw before. That she did not have a drawing of him was also strange for some reason.

As it turned out, the Crow brave was not one from the renegade camp. He came to invite Chief Sitting Bull and Chief Red Cloud to a meeting of Indian chiefs that the soldiers at Laramie had planned. His chief wanted Sitting Bull to know first about it before the soldiers came to tell him. He wanted them to get together first and talk before they went to the white man's meeting.

Grandfather agreed to give that exact message to Chief Sitting Bull.

What Grandfather's old eyes had not noticed, but Jane Ann's young ones had, was the brave sitting on his horse just to the edge of the camp. He had not come in like the lone rider had. Jane Ann wondered why.

Jane Ann then walked straight toward the figure sitting there on his horse. How strange that two Crow braves would ride up to camp but only one ride in. As she got nearer to the rider, he suddenly turned and started to ride away. She was disappointed. Some hope deep inside her had wanted that rider to be Bear Claw. Sadly, she turned and started back to her tipi.

If that had been Bear Claw, he would have ridden into camp himself to give the message to his uncle and cousin. She knew that moment she was being a fool and that she had better agree to marry Red Cloud or else find some way back to England. She was beginning to doubt herself, that she knew what was right, so maybe she needed to return to where she came from and start over!

Then the Crow rider turned his horse and slowly made his way toward the same tipi the girl was heading for. She had a limp so obvious it was painful to watch her make her way such a distance. He thought about picking her up, putting her on his horse, and riding away with her. Instead, he watched her enter the tipi and close the entrance. For just a few minutes he waited, then he dismounted and walked toward the tipi.

As he entered the tipi, Jane Ann turned and without hesitation breathed, "You! I was hoping it was you, Bear Claw!" Tears were streaming down her face. "So long, why did you wait so long?" She fairly jumped into his arms.

He was moved by her greeting, so different from what he expected. Many times he had dreamed of this moment during the past year. He had dreamed of holding her close like this, of feeling her woman's body next to his, of feeling her breathing against his face. This was crazy and he knew it was, but he had put off their reunion long enough.

Finally all her tears were spent and Jane Ann relaxed her hold on Bear Claw. "I'm sorry to have acted like a girl," she began and then blushed. "Can you stay?" She did not know what to say, what to ask him, how not to scare him off.

"Wait," he answered, "I only came to get a look at you from a distance. I didn't plan on holding you again. I've dreamed of our meeting but I never dared hope you would want to." He paused.

"I did not either. I mean I did not know either that I would ever want to see you again. But, Bear Claw, you saved my life! How could I forget that? How could I just disappear and never say thank you?"

Another voice spoke from the doorway. "Yes," Grandfather said, "Your life has been saved by Red Cloud, too." He reminded her, "Who also wants you for his wife. Will you expect this Indian to want you for his wife, too?"

Jane Ann began crying. She could not believe Grandfather would be so cruel to her. Yet he had spoken from his heart. Perhaps it was she who was cruel. She had been cruel to Red Cloud by refusing to answer whether she would marry him or not. She had been cruel to Bear Claw by ignoring him for a year and now wanting him to come and reunite with her. Then an awful thought came across her mind. What if her silly girlish way were to make enemies of these cousins? They did not deserve such dishonor especially when both of them had saved her life. She owed them both her life. She had to talk to them both honestly together at the same time.

"Stay awhile until Red Cloud returns." Jane Ann asked Bear Claw. "Stay because I want to talk to both of you. It is very important to me." Her eyes were pleading.

Bear Claw nodded. He bent his head and then turned and walked out with Grandfather.

Jane Ann had to think. She had to be clear what she was going to say to the two of them together. She had to weigh her words carefully.

By the time Red Cloud returned and he and Bear Claw came to enter her tent, Jane Ann had propped and pinned about 30 drawings around all sides. When they walked in, a panorama of faces greeted them. Jane Ann had to put them out so she could see what in her life was important and what was not. She wanted to be very sure about who she was and what she wanted for the rest of her days before she talked to these two strong warriors, these two good men who loved her. She also loved them both, but she wasn't sure until she pinned all the pictures where she could look at them, exactly which one she would choose to spend her life with. By the time they walked in to hear her, she knew which one.

It was breathtaking to enter where so many faces looked back at you! Both Red Cloud and Bear Claw now knew that Jane Ann had a gift for reflecting a person's Spirit in her drawings. Red Cloud stopped before the drawing of him and wondered that she could see his spirit better than he ever had himself. Bear Claw paused at the drawing of himself and, instead of deceitful eyes and an angry mouth, he saw strength in the face before him, and vision and hope in the eyes. Jane Ann had a way of seeing deep into the real person.

The two men walked around the tipi looking at drawings of other Indians, of Grandfather and Rena, of Rain and Chief Sitting Bull. There were many of children, and of boat captains, of people going about the streets of St. Louis and New York and London. There were drawings of Mama and Papa, of Grandmother Rogers, and of Uncle Percy and Aunt Agnes, and of Tillie and Petrie and Grace. Over the last few years and in the years before coming to America, Jane Ann had been drawing the faces of the people in her life. It was a breathtaking display!

Then Grandfather and Rena both stood, unable to move, transfixed before the drawing of a beautiful Indian woman in a white dress. Red Cloud, looking past their shoulders, smiled as he looked at the familiar face of White Buffalo Woman from his own visions.

Jane Ann let them look as long as they wanted. Then she tried to draw their attention back to what she had asked them here for. "I need to talk to you both, Red Cloud and Bear Claw, so you will understand why I am having such a hard time making a choice what to do with my life." She held up her hand when Grandfather tried to speak. "Shush, let me speak, please, I may not have courage later." Then she turned back to Red Cloud and Bear Claw.

"I love many of the people I have drawn in these pictures. But now I am a woman and I am faced with choosing who I want to be my husband and my partner, the father of my children. I love you both equally for saving my life. You saved me from dying in the snow, Red Cloud, and then you saved me again from the Crow." She gently reached to touch his face. Then she turned to Bear Claw.

"You, Bear Claw, saved me from being, only Spirit knows what, perhaps tortured and killed by Sheffield or the Crow." She gently touched Bear Claw's face. Then she walked around to stand beside Rena. "I love both of you fine men equally for saving my life. I love you equally as my friends. But I choose you only, Bear Claw, as my husband and the father of my children." She lowered her head, not wanting then to look at either of them, not daring to look around her at the disappointment she would see in anyone's face. She had made the decision and now she must stand or fall by it. She was afraid.

Red Cloud spoke first. "I hear you and I know you speak from your heart, Jane Ann," he took a step toward her. "I knew long ago it would not be me you would choose, yet I knew even then that you love me, too." He drew her hand over to Bear Claw and placed it in his.

"I am happy for you, Bear Claw," Red Cloud smiled warmly, "Even though I am jealous and I still want her for my own, I am pleased she chose one of us. Just look at the faces around us in the paintings. She could have chosen anyone!" He paused a moment and then added, "Oh, yes, Bear Claw and Jane Ann, you may come and live in my camp and be with me always."

Bear Claw nodded and he held Jane Ann's hand gently. He knew life would be different from this day forward. There would be no more living with and pretending to be Crow. He looked at Jane Ann and nodded again for her to say what she wanted. She smiled and whispered, "Yes!"

Then Bear Claw looked at Red Cloud and with a smile said, "We accept. We will come and be members of your camp, Chief Red Cloud. Thank you, my cousin."

"Come soon, before the Winter snows start." Red Cloud answered. Then he went to gather his braves and leave.

Grandfather and Rena were beside themselves with happiness. They set out to spread the word over the whole camp. There would be a wedding pretty soon. Grandfather walked toward Chief Sitting Bull's tipi to tell him that Bear Claw had come home and that he and Jane Ann were going to be husband and wife. What a good day it was!

CHAPTER 16

The fire had not burned down the trading post after all. The stables had caught ablaze because someone turned over a lamp that was lit. There was little damage to the building itself. Everyone from Sitting Bull's camp had come back satisfied they had done a good job helping the trader.

Sitting Bull was very happy also to hear that Bear Claw had returned and that he and Jane Ann were going to get married. He had not known that Jane Ann even knew Bear Claw so it was a great surprise to him. He'd thought she was going to be Red Cloud's second wife. Things work out for the best for everyone, so it seems.

The meeting with the chiefs and then the meeting with the white Cavalry at Fort Laramie would be another matter. Since they had the trading post active again, and had finished building the fort at Laramie, Sitting Bull assumed the white man was here to stay. So he began thinking of ways they could all live in peace together.

This is what he and Red Cloud talked about before Red Cloud went back to his Camp later that afternoon. They agreed immediately they would go to the Chiefs' Meeting together. Also they'd maybe even attend the Laramie meeting together. There must be peace for their peoples. The land was big enough for all.

Red Cloud was wondering about that though. He had looked carefully at the drawings of the cities Jane Ann had hanging in her tipi. The ones of London, Boston, St. Louis all showed the streets crowded with people going this way and that. If there were that many white people, he wondered if there would be enough land in the west for them all.

"We have to learn more about them," Sitting Bull agreed, "Maybe even buy some of their hats from the Trading Post, maybe even dress like them, too." He was thinking secretly that he would not mind wearing one of the hats.

In the meantime, Bear Claw and Jane Ann were sitting together in her tipi. Earlier both of them had been wondering if they would ever see each other again. Now she could touch him and he could hold her when they pleased.

"I did not dare dream of having you as my wife," Bear Claw began.

"I think you had in mind something else, like having me as your love slave," Jane Ann teased him, remembering then his own teasing words from over a year ago.

They both laughed remembering being in the tipi together a week without touching except in the water. "And when you kissed me goodbye," she reminded him.

He looked at her drawings in the darkness of the tipi. "I look at all these people and wonder about you, Jane Ann," Bear Claw said softly, "How can you choose me from all the men you have known before?" He sounded truly puzzled.

Jane Ann turned and kissed him warmly, then held him, clinging to him as she brushed her lips against his cheek, "I have waited all my life to know you, Bear Claw, and I plan on giving you at least a dozen sons!"

Their wedding ceremony was a beautiful ritual Jane Ann was nervous about but very glad to have over. Rena had made her a beautiful white dress with fringe hanging from the sleeves and skirt. Wherever she walked the fringe would sway softly back and forth giving her a soft feminine look. Grandfather would say later that the dress looked very similar to the one Jane Ann had drawn on White Buffalo Woman in her picture. Rena nodded with a smile.

Bear Claw had been nervous as a bear in a trap. Red Cloud and Rain came with him so he would not run away. "If you so much as look in another direction than Jane Ann," Red Cloud had threatened, "I will scoop her up on my pony and ride off with her."

Rain threatened to do the same thing. "Do not be nervous. Do not run away!" he had cautioned Bear Claw.

"It's not Jane Ann I'm afraid of, you two" Bear Claw had affirmed, "It's everybody else watching and looking at me. Just like you are doing right now!"

"Forget everybody else!" Red Cloud answered gruffly. "Just go get her and leave. Go to the hideaway tipi I told you about and stay there at least three days."

"Or as long as you want," Rain added.

Red Cloud nodded. "Then come on to my camp. You will have the biggest tipi in camp other than my own, of course."

Somehow they all made it through the wedding ceremony. Actually, it was not as long as Jane Ann thought it would be and she was happy about that. They bade Rena and Grandfather and Chief Sitting Bull farewell, then nodded to Red Cloud and Rain and the others, and they were off to start their life together.

Their time in the mountains together was so beautiful, neither of them would ever forget. Red Cloud and Rain had placed their tipi secretly near a waterfall. No one else would know where to find it but Jane Ann and Bear Claw. The waterfall was the first thing they both saw as they came out of the tipi each morning. In the evening, they would hear the water falling. It was a peaceful and healing place. The flowers bloomed all over the ground. Jane Ann saw many birds she'd never seen before. It was like Red Cloud and Rain had found paradise for them to enjoy.

Every day Bear Claw would pick her a handful of lavender flowers and wake her with their smell by putting them right by her face.

One morning, Jane Ann awoke with a headache and later she envisioned White Buffalo Woman showing them a beautiful baby boy. She knew then that she and Bear Claw would have a son, and this made them both very happy.

By the time they returned and went to live in Red Cloud's camp, Red Cloud had gone to the Chiefs' Meeting with Sitting Bull and returned. The chiefs had talked endlessly about getting rid of the whites, of killing them as they came into the territory, of surrounding Laramie and burning it to the ground, all sorts of ways to get rid of the white man. Sitting Bull, wearing a white man's hat, told them "No" that he would not let his people fight in a war against the white man. He and Red Cloud had seen streets filled with white people and the two of them knew the Indian would not have enough knives, arrows or bullets to kill all the whites. A lot of screaming and yelling was done then. Nobody agreed on anything. They did not even appoint a leader to make decisions. They argued until they finally started getting up and leaving.

"The Council Meeting of Chiefs did not go well at all," was all that Red Cloud had to say. He tried and tried to think of something he could do, something maybe he and Sitting Bull could do to bring peace. Finally he hit on the idea of going to Laramie and sitting down and talking with the white leaders. Maybe even to get them to have their higher leaders sit down and talk to Chief Sitting Bull. Eventually, maybe they could all sit down in peace together and decide who was going to live where and then just do it! Anywhere but in their sacred Black Hills Pa Sapa.

Then, without anybody knowing, somebody in Red Cloud's camp stole some of Jane Ann's paintings and drawings of Indians and took them to the Trading Post. The clerk there said he could sell them to make a lot of money for the Indian. The Indian must have forgotten that the man was a crook and a liar. The Indian got paid $1.00 and a dirty blanket for six drawings of Indians.

Later, the clerk then sold the drawings to a prospector who was going into the Black Hills looking for gold. The prospector sold the drawings to a Bank Manager back in St. Louis the following year. About three years later after then, the drawings ended up in the hands of a detective. That detective had a Missing Persons Report with a description of an English family that had left London in 1852 heading for Sioux territory who had never been seen or heard from since leaving St. Louis in a covered wagon. The name on the drawings was the same as one of the names on the Report: Jane Ann Rogers. The report further said a large reward would be given to anyone with information about where to find anyone in the family of Harold Chance Rogers, Emma Ann Peterson Rogers (his wife), and Jane Ann Rogers (their daughter).

"If you have any information," the Report read, "Please contact Percy Dodge Rogers, M.D. or his wife, Agnes de Paul Rogers, at the address below, or telegraph (Collect) to a number in London, England."

The detective, Murphy Pierson, sent a collect telegram to Dr. Percy Dodge Rogers in London, England immediately telling him that some drawings by Miss Jane Ann Rogers had recently surfaced in the City of St. Louis. Miss Rogers had been traced heading for Sioux Indian territory with her family in the year 1852 late November. He asked if any further instructions were forthcoming.

Within hours, a wire was received from the Law Firm of Dudley, Dudley and Fitch in London, England, directing Detective Murphy Pierson to set out immediately for Sioux territory seeking to find the aforementioned Miss Jane Ann Rogers and return her safely to Boston, Massachusetts, U.S.A. from where she will directly be chaperoned to the nearest port and return home to London. A sum of $2,000.00 American dollars was made available for any expenses Detective Pierson might incur. He was to furnish an itemized list of any such expenditures, of course, to the aforementioned Dudley, Dudley and Fitch, Attorneys at Law.

That was all Pierson needed to get going. If this was a down payment, then Dr. Percy Rogers was probably willing to pay a lot of money for the return of his family.

Jane Ann knew nothing about the detective or the missing persons report that had been circulating all those years among various law enforcement agencies all the way from London, England, to San Francisco, California. She also had not yet discovered that some of her drawings were missing.

Jane Ann and Bear Claw welcomed a baby son into the world on November 11, 1858. They named him Harold and waited until he was older and walking, as was Sioux custom, to give him his Indian name.

Rena came to live with Jane Ann and the new baby while Bear Claw went with Red Cloud to meetings and gatherings where the Indian was trying to decide what to do about the whites moving in. The white man at the Trading Post had already told them the government was planning on building a railroad across the Sioux territory. He said they planned to stretch it on across other Indian tribal lands all the way to California. They already had plans to lay telegraph line across the same direction. He predicted the place would be crawling with whites in no time.

That's when the crooked trader began trying to "buy" land from any Indian that came into the Trading Post. Unfortunately, there were a few Indians who sold land but they failed to get rich at the price of 75 cents an acre that the white clerk was paying.

One day, Red Cloud decided to take things into his hands and take a few good Braves with him and go to Laramie to talk with the Captain of the cavalry. Sitting Bull thought it was a good idea, too, but he let Red Cloud go alone that time with just a few braves so as not to frighten the white men.

On their journey to the fort, another cavalry regiment which was on the way for duty at the fort, happened to come across Red Cloud and his small band of braves. They had been frightened of meeting any Indians head on and the Officer in charge decided to shoot them all and then he would not have to be afraid anymore. Red Cloud tried to talk to them. The whites started shooting at the little band and the next thing they knew, nineteen of the white cavalry had been killed. As the soldiers were stretched on the ground bleeding and dying, Red Cloud counted the bodies and there were 19. It was then, as the rest of the cavalry regiment was fleeing in the distance, that Red Cloud remembered White Buffalo Woman had warned them about this very incident. Jane Ann had warned them that night long ago around Sitting Bull's campfire.

When Red Cloud returned to camp, he found Jane Ann drawing Harry playing with the puppy in the camp. Red Cloud walked up and stood behind her for awhile watching her charcoal move back and forth creating first lines, then filling them in, until suddenly images appeared.

"He is a fine boy," Red Cloud mused as he watched Harry pat the puppy gently once on the head and then run quickly away, then sit down and laugh like he had just counted coup.

"Oh, Red Cloud," Jane Ann stood up, "There you are. We wondered how long you would be at the Fort. Did things go well?"

She watched as his eyes changed from joy to sadness. "No," he shook his head. "Do you remember the night at Sitting Bull's campfire when White Buffalo Woman showed me and a small party of braves going to talk to the captain at Laramie, and another cavalry came and attacked us, then we fought back and killed 19 white men?"

Jane Ann nodded. She did remember.

"That is where I have come from. We never made it to Laramie." He watched the boy playing and laughing. He wondered if one day the whole problem would be solved not by wars, not by grown men talking, but by little children like him being born. Little redskins with red hair! But he didn't say it out loud.

Jane Ann stood up and put her hand up on Red Cloud's shoulder. "I am sorry, that vision frightened me then and it still does." She paused. "Do you remember the rest of what White Buffalo Woman showed us?"

He nodded. "An even bigger cavalry of white men raiding a Sioux village and killing everybody they can find, up to a hundred Sioux. It was to make us pay for killing 19 of their soldiers." He stared even harder now at the ground.

Jane Ann shivered, "And arresting the chief and putting him in prison."

They both stood silent a moment. Jane didn't know which camp would be attacked or which chief imprisoned. She shivered again.

"Go, Jane Ann, take the child and find Bear Claw. Send him to me, please," Red Cloud said.

Jane Ann picked up Harry and took him to Rena and then she went to find Bear Claw. He was supposed to be down at the creek gathering stones to help Grandfather with the medicine fire later. But she could not find him. Only a young brave was there and he told Jane Ann that Bear Claw went to the Trading Post.

That seemed strange at the time because he had said nothing to her about having to go to the Trading Post today, but then, he didn't always tell her everything. She went back and took a pony out of the corral and got on and rode toward the Trading Post in search of Bear Claw. It was not a long ride and she was soon there.

But she could not find Bear Claw's pony out front. There were wagons there though. She went in to ask the clerk if he had seen Bear Claw. By now, the clerk knew most of the people from their camp since they were located nearby. Everyone stared at her, the women looking as if they just smelled something bad, the men with more interest than they should have had. She always disliked going into the Trading Post.

"Mr. Binder," Jane Ann began, "Have you seen Bear Claw today?"

"Nope, not today, Mrs. Bear Claw," he always sounded sarcastic like an actor on the stage doing bad lines. "But I got someone here who wants to meet you real bad. He says he knows your Uncle in London, Dr. Rogers."

Jane Ann was startled. "Uncle Percy?" she asked not believing her ears. "Who is it?"

"This gent here is Detective Murphy Pierson lately from St. Louis. He has a telegram from your Uncle asking that you come with him to Boston. What do you think about that?" He grinned as if he had known something she did not know.

Jane Ann looked at Detective Pierson. "Do you know my Uncle?" she asked again. The man nodded. "Can I see some proof of your identity, please? And whatever you have that might prove that you know Uncle Percy." She accepted the papers he was handing her. He had small beady eyes and he was chewing tobacco. Something about him made her remember Sheffield. It was all she could do to look him in the face but she did. She read through the MISSING PERSON REPORT, the telegram copy to Uncle Percy from Detective Pierson, and the reply from Dudley, Dudley and Fitch. It all looked legal but it might have been bunk. However, she would have to talk this over long and hard with Bear Claw and Red Cloud. Of course, Bear Claw and Harry would go with her. She was trying to think of everything and she didn't even hear the clerk say in a snide voice: "You ain't going to be so uppity, little crippled girl, where you're going now, is she Mr. Pierson?" And then someone hit her hard up side her head. She blacked out immediately.

CHAPTER 17

Jane Ann woke up to find herself bound hand and foot, blindfolded, and lying on her side in a moving wagon. At first she thought she was back in the Crow camp and she was three and a half years younger. Then she remembered Bear Claw and Harry. And the snippy clerk in the Trading Post, and Detective Pierson!

"Who are you?" Jane Ann asked. "Where are you taking me?" She could smell tobacco and whiskey, and she started shivering.

A hand reached down and patted her arm and moved across her chest. She hit at it as hard as she could with her shoulder. The hand slapped her across the mouth.

"Stop being so damned hard to get along with." Detective Pierson drawled and spit a mouthful of tobacco juice high so the wind blew it back into his face. He wiped his face with his arm and cursed a few times. "You and I are going to be great friends before this trip is finished, little lady, yes maam, great friends."

"Where are you taking me?" She demanded to know.

"To Boston, maam, to Boston like the telegram says. There we're going to get you a chaperone." At that point he giggled like a schoolboy. "one who will escort you to a ship to take you to England and your Uncle." Then he added, "I'm going to be rich because of you, rich and maybe famous, too. I saw those drawings of yours and they're pretty good. I'm going to sell them and retire. Lots of people are getting interested in Indians nowadays. I know at least two old crows with a bank full of money who'd pay me lots for just one picture apiece."

137

Jane Ann didn't say anything. She was trying to think clearly but it was hard because her head hurt bad. If only she could get free of her ropes, "and take this infernal blindfold off my eyes!" she said the last part out loud.

He guffawed at that. "You want to see where you're going, maam?" he asked. "I wonder if you still will when we get there. There's lots of men who are going to pay me lots of money to get their hands on you tonight. I might even be rich after we make this stop and forget the rest of the trip."

"My Uncle won't like that at all, Pierson," she replied, hoping he would think very carefully before doing anything as stupid as whatever he was insinuating.

"White woman with red hair living with an Indian, there ain't no telling how long, how many of them red men do you think I know had their hands on you already? A few white men won't make no difference." He spit again and it landed again in his face. He got mad just thinking about it! "Bet you got some red babies out of the deal, too. We just going to have to find them and kill them, you know. We can't have no mixing of the races. It ain't Christian." He laughed then like had just said something funny.

"Mr. Pierson, you think hard about it. My Uncle is a doctor in London, a very successful one. He can pay you a lot of money, but he won't pay you a cent if you don't bring me back safe. Why do you think he is going to have a chaperone waiting in Boston to accompany me to the ship?" For a long time, the man did not say anything. Jane Ann said, "Just tell me how much more you can make off me than my Uncle can pay you? She had given him something to think about anyway. She began to pull harder at the ropes. There had to be a way she could get loose.

Suddenly he jerked the wagon to a stop. He jumped off and came around and untied her. He unbound her eyes. For a minute she couldn't see anything except stars. The sun was shining so bright she had to blink a few times. Finally his face came into focus. Her shirt had pulled open where two buttons were now missing.

"I think you got a nursing brat," he leered

Her face turned crimson and she tried to turn away from him.

"You got an ugly leg there, too. I watched you walk in all crippled like. I wonder what that'll be worth to your doctor Uncle, them reds mutilating you like that, it's a shame." He grabbed her and brought her face up close to his.

She felt like throwing up in his face, and wished she could. The smell of tobacco and whiskey made her even sicker. He had the same brown ooze at the corners of his mouth as Sheffield had. She shivered.

"You're a little thing, though, and sassy." He hauled her up and out of the wagon. "Me and you got to get friendly real quick so I can decide what to do here." He walked around her feeling of her arm and her back, at everywhere he could feel, as if he were checking hanging beef.

Jane Ann knew she could be in danger. She did not want to die but she didn't want to leave Bear Claw and Harry. "I do have a baby, Mr. Pierson," she said suddenly sounding polite in a quiet and pleading voice, "I do have a husband, duly married and all, and I'm a good Christian woman, never been with a man other than my husband, never want to either!" She was watching his face. "You cannot take me unless you kill me first. I will fight you and whatever mark you make on me is going to cost you a great deal of money." She must have hit a nerve because he stopped leering at her. "Every mark is going to be one more reason for Uncle Percy to have you arrested in Boston."

He stopped and moved back a step.

Jane Ann continued talking. "I imagine the chaperone in Boston will have orders to check me over pretty good. I speak quite well, Mr. Pierson, and even if you cut out my tongue, I can still draw pictures showing what you did to me."

He tightened up his mouth and balled up his fist.

"And if you cut off my hands so I cannot draw, I can scream and scream it until somebody knows what you've done to me, you bastard! She was screaming now at the top of her lungs. With all her might, she spat straight into his face.

He didn't move for a second and she did. She climbed up fast onto the wagon and took off quick. She didn't know what direction to go in but she flew as fast as she could for as long as she could. Before nightfall she came across a Trading Post. She went in and the clerk there told her she was in Missouri very close, perhaps an hour away from St. Louis. A carriage usually came through every evening about this time if she wanted to go to St. Louis that way.

It would be about a week before a carriage or mail wagon came through heading to Sioux territory. However, he told her, she might get something quicker out of St. Louis to the territories. So, she asked if he would give her a ticket on the carriage in swap for the wagon she came in. He nodded and said it was a good deal for him, that she would have cash money left over. She thanked him and put the money in her pocket. At last she could sit down and draw a breath, and wait for the carriage to come.

Once in St. Louis, she immediately asked the clerk in the railroad for a way to return back to Sioux Indian territory and was told that every day at least one mail wagon left headed that way. It would be months before the railroad was finished that far West though. The man told her to come back at 10:00 o'clock the next morning and he would make sure she got on one of the wagons. She nodded agreement, paid him what he told her it cost, and told him she would be back.

As she was walking out the door of the station, she smelled wet tobacco and whiskey. She looked up in time to see Detective Pierson. He put his arm across in front of her and he would not let her pass. He shook his head NO.

"Now, dearie, you and me, we got to finish our little trip. Your Uncle is waiting and he sure wants you back home. Just let me help you on to where we are going to sleep tonight. I bet you are hungry for a bite to eat. Sweet little thing, you are, now, now, let's go." He droned on and on attempting to sound like a husband whose wife is trying to get away from him. "She may have had one drink too many," he nodded to passers-by, "and she can't walk too good now, poor thing." He had her held tight now, his arm around her shoulders. "You ain't going to get away again, believe that." He whispered in a low voice, "No, maam, not again!"

He took her to a cheap hotel where loud music was playing downstairs. He got a key from the clerk and practically dragged her upstairs to a dirty room, then he opened the door and threw her in. "You better be here when I come back," he warned her, "or I will cut you into little pieces myself." He squeezed her arm and twisted it behind her. Then he threw her down on the bed and turned and left. At the door he turned and said, "Oh, and I will tell your Uncle it was your dear husband who cut you into little pieces. Yes, he will believe me. There are awful stories about Indians all over the place." He stared at her awhile. "Especially tales about what they do to white women." He pursed his lips and came back, and then he leaned close to her face. "See, I can do anything to you and blame it on them. You better be good to me, girl!" Then he turned and went out and slammed the door, and she heard the key turn. She was locked in!

Later, he came back upstairs and unlocked the door. He threw a cotton dress at her and told her to change clothes. She did as he said. Then he smiled, "You don't look half bad when you got clothes on." He took her by the arm and roughly pushed her toward the hallway and the stairs.

"Where are we going?" She asked him.

"To eat, maam, to eat. I got to feed you now so you won't be too skinny when you get home to your Uncle. Don't want that, no maam."

Maybe (Jane thought) there will be some way to get free from him while eating.

"Don't you worry your little head, girl, you ain't escaping from me again, and I mean it!" He squeezed her arm hard and she let out a yelp.

People sitting at tables looked up at them. Jane Ann's hair was wild looking, red curls thick and matted and sticking out all over. She felt like she must look a sight. But she didn't care about how she looked. She just wanted to get away. He walked her over to a table in the corner and ordered her to sit down.

The minute he took his hand off her arm, she leaped away and ran as fast as she could away from him. She ran straight into the arms of a man coming out of the back gambling room and almost knocked him off his feet.

"Whoa!" the man laughed, "Where are you going in such a hurry?" he asked her while grabbing her arms at the same time to steady her. Then he bowed politely. "My name is . . ." he started but she didn't hear him because Pierson was right behind her and she could feel him going to grab her arm again. As they both took off through the swinging door into the gambling room, the doors swung back and the well dressed man caught hold, standing there, watching them.

"I declare," he said mostly to himself. "That girl sure does look familiar." He wondered if he had slept with her somewhere up or down the river. He watched carefully as the man caught up with the girl and swung her around. He began beating her about the face and upper body.

Without a second thought, gambler and ladies' man, George Lee Anderson, dashed in to save the lady. He gave Pierson a sound enough beating to keep him down while someone went and got the sheriff. The Sheriff reluctantly took him to jail. George finally convinced him if he didn't, the man would probably kill the woman. Then George bent over to pick up the girl.

"My dear," George said, "You really are a mess, you know." Then as he carried her upstairs to his room, he said, "Oh, by the way, my name is George Lee Anderson, late of Boston, formerly of London, England." He looked at her carefully. "I doubt that you've heard of London though." Then he opened the door with his key and set her down gently. "You may want to bathe, the water's over there," he pointed to a tub filled with soapy water. "Well, do you have a name? Or am I supposed to guess?"

Jane Ann took a deep breath. She was still dizzy from being hit so many times, But she could have sworn the well dressed man said his name was George Lee Anderson.

"I am Jane Ann," she said, not giving her identity away too soon. If someone like Pierson knew about money being paid by her Uncle for finding her, then this well dressed gambler probably did, too.

"Ha," he said, "I knew a Jane Ann once. She was a lovely creature. She had long red curls and was tiny and sweet and . . . . but you could not be her."

"Do you have a twin sister named Georgette?" Jane Ann asked quietly.

George looked puzzled. "Yes, of course, but how do you know that?"

"I don't know, George, maybe it's because you and your sister and I came over from London, England, on the same ship into New York harbor. Maybe because she and I became great friends, and I thought you and I were friends, too. By the way, do you still have the drawing I did of the three of us? The one I copied so we each would have one? Maybe because we are supposed to keep journals of our experiences in America and share them someday."

George was smiling, standing there almost catatonic, unable to get the silly look off his face. He could hardly believe his ears. He felt as if he was moving in slow motion. He started to laugh. "God bless us all!" he laughed until Jane Ann feared his sides would split. "You really are Jane Ann Rogers!" He looked at her again with a smile. "I told you we would meet again," he made a comic gesture of bowing to royalty "and here we are, two ships in the night. Familiar ships, right?" He was laughing again.

She turned in mock surprise. He was a fine gentleman! Well, at least he had saved her life, and she could stand the teasing. She got into the bath and took her time bathing and washing her hair.

He gradually stopped laughing like a hyena, and slowly he sat down on the bed and began watching her intently. "By jove, you are Jane Ann!" He breathed out a long sigh "I cannot wait to tell Georgette."

"Is she here?" Jane Ann asked while thinking she would really know if she was dreaming if Georgette were here, too.

"No, of course not, she is married, living back in Boston, and is very much the merry matron with a bevy of little Georgettes. But, I'm going back in two weeks and I will tell her how I found you." George said, and then asked, "How have I found you, by the way?" Who was that man? Where are you heading to? What is going on in your life, dear girl?

Jane Ann didn't know where to start. There were so many questions! She grabbed a big towel and got out of the tub. She felt better now that she was clean. She hoped to goodness that she never saw that idiot, Pierson, again.

"Jane Ann," George asked, "Who is that dreadful man I had hauled off to jail? Is he your husband or lover or something?" George did not want to get into trouble with anybody else's husband, as he'd already had a bit of experience with that.

"No, of course not. My husband and my son are back in Indian Territory in the Black Hills area." She was trying desperately to comb the tangles out of her hair with little success.

George walked over and said, "Sit down, silly, if I can get Georgette's hair smooth, surely I can do yours." He began to brush it rather well, and so Jane Ann let him.

"Say, George, I've got to send a telegram to my Uncle in London. Can you help me?" Jane Ann asked.

"Oh, yes, that will be easy. There's a telegraph office downstairs just next door. We can send it right away as soon as you get your clothes on."

Jane Ann realized she was sitting in a hotel room in a strange town with a man she had not seen since he was 17 years old and she was 15, and here she was, a grown woman dressed only in a towel. "What a sight I must be!" she added.

"Yes, you look like a street girl all bruised up like that," he agreed. "But your hair is well brushed now. There!" He gave her his brush and watched her look in the mirror. "Say, that's a nasty cut there over your eye. My dear, you must promise me not to take up boxing; you would be killed the first time in the ring." He laughed at his own joke.

143

"George, I need a dress, undergarments, and shoes if you don't mind." She looked at him and he smiled.

"Alright, I can do that." George nodded. He looked at her as if sizing her. She was at least two sizes smaller than Georgette.

"And, then I need you to escort me down to the Telegraph Office to send Uncle a telegram. Then would you help me get back to the Indian territories?" Her eyes begged him.

He nodded, "Yes, yes, and no." Then he added, "I cannot go into the Indian Territories. They are having a bit of a mess out there right now. Shooting and killing and all that. It is dangerous. Everyone who does not have business there is being asked to wait until the cavalry has everything under control. Haven't you heard what's going on, Jane Ann?" He wondered why she didn't know what everyone was talking about.

She shook her head.'no.'

"Awhile back, a Sioux chief named Red Cloud killed some Cavalry men who were out on patrol near Fort Laramie. Then recently, in retaliation, the Cavalry went to an Indian village and killed nearly every Indian there. Everybody within hundreds of miles of the place is scared to death. Anybody who walks the wrong way in the territories is in danger from both the Indians and the Cavalry!"

Jane Ann turned pale. "What Indian village? Where is the camp they killed so many people in, George? Please! I have to know. My husband and son are out there somewhere." Her face was ashen, and she was shaking like a leaf. She looked as if she were going to faint.

"I believe one of the papers said it was Red Cloud's camp somewhere near a river. However, I heard he got away." She was trembling, and George suddenly felt sorry for her. "Jane Ann, this is a big country, and it doesn't mean your husband and child are dead just because some Indian village is gone to dust. Think of the odds, girl!"

Jane Ann started crying. "Yes, George, I know what you mean, but think of the odds of me running into you in a café tonight in St. Louis." He nodded. She looked up at him, "George, my husband is Sioux Indian, and we live in Red Cloud's camp."

"My word, Jane Ann, we have a real problem here." He put his arm around her shoulders and patted her gently. He didn't know quite what to do.

CHAPTER 18

As soon as George brought Jane Ann's new clothes to her, she dressed quickly. She tried every way she knew to cover her bruises as thoroughly as possible, but she had no make up to help her. Then they went downstairs to the Telegraph Office. Jane Ann first sent a telegram to her Uncle Percy in London informing him that the Detective Pierson he hired was a sadistic fraud who had kidnapped her away from her husband and son, and who had planned to hold her prisoner for a large ransom. She further told Percy that Emma and Harold had died in the mountains in an avalanche on their way to Indian territory, while she had been rescued by Sioux Indians. She had been living with them the past four years until that fraud, Pierson, had kidnapped and beaten her. She asked for help keeping Pierson in jail, and from him contacting her in any way. She also asked for money so that she could return to Sioux territory and try to find her husband and child.

The telegraph clerk acted surprised that anyone would want to send such a long message, but when George insisted, he sent it as she directed him to.

"But, it will cost you over $9.00 American money," the clerk had insisted.

"Give it to him, please, George." Jane Ann said while ignoring the clerk's rude manner.

George smiled amiably. "Of course, my dear." Then he reached over and put his face close to the clerk's. George said, "The message is worth the money, but the insults are not!"

The clerk coughed and said, "Well, I declare!"

145

Jane Ann and George stayed in the Telegraph Office waiting for an answer. They were not disappointed. About an hour and a few minutes later, a long answer came back from London. It was addressed to Jane Ann Rogers with love from Percy Dodge Rogers, M.D. The message read:

> Thank God I have found you, my dear Jane Ann. (Stop) My sympathies (Stop) I urge you to return to find husband and son immediately (Stop) All then come to London (Stop) Account in your name First Bank of of St. Louis (Stop) Have no concerns about Pierson, Sheriff there being contacted this minute by Dudley, Dudley and Fitch (Stop) Anxious to see you (Stop) Loving Regards from Your Uncle Percy

"Well, I do believe that ties up all the loose ends now, Jane Ann." George beamed as he read the message over her shoulder. "Let's go for a bite to eat at the café and then check in at the First Bank of St. Louis and see how well off you are, that is, if they are still open this late. Then you can decide whether to hire a personal bodyguard and a guide, or to travel with the Cavalry back into the Indian territories. How's that for solving the whole thing?"

The telegraph clerk cleared his throat. "Pardon, Maam," he nodded to Jane Ann. "Haven't you heard about most of the Cavalry being called back East? There's a war brewing and they are needed to keep the peace."

George nodded at Jane Ann in sympathy. They went to the Café then and George got a copy of the Boston Globe Newspaper while Jane Ann ordered them something to eat for supper. She was beginning to feel very tired but she didn't say anything to George. It was George who handed Jane Ann the key and insisted she go up to the room and get a good night's sleep.

"I am going to read the Globe here, Jane Ann, and then see how lucky I am in the game room. I dare say, I will spend the night in there as I usually do. You, my Lady, need to go rest in peace." Then he added, "I sleep naps during the day."

Finally, after sipping warm tea and toast, she agreed and went upstairs where she slept too soundly most of the night until just before daylight.

George, meanwhile, was reading page 2 of the Boston Globe Newspaper, about the Civil War beginning back East all the while an Indian uprising was beginning in the territories. The writer listed a number of raids on white people, some murders of children, and other incidents by the Indians. And then the writer proceeded to describe the Cavalry's destruction of Red Cloud's village in retaliation for the Indian uprising. George frowned as he read that article. Somehow, it did not make sense to him that a person like Jane Ann would be married to a bloodthirsty savage, much less living with murdering people for four years or more, even if they had saved her life! George was thinking who ever wrote that article probably never left the City of Boston! He could only wonder how many people reading such an article believed even one of them was the truth!

The next day, Jane Ann discovered that Uncle Percy had put more than sufficient funds at her disposal, no matter whether she took a short time or the whole rest of her life to find her family and get back to England. Jane Ann and George stopped by the Sheriff's office and discovered that Pierson had been moved to a prison in another territory where he was wanted on escape charges. It did not sound like he would be any trouble to her at all. The Sheriff was quite cooperative even when Jane Ann expressed her need for a guide to take her into Indian territory.

"That's not a good idea right now, maam," the Sheriff had said kindly. "There is a lot going on out there now that is not safe for a woman. It would be hard to find anyone trustworthy to take you anyway. It is just plain hard for a woman traveling alone with a man.

"Well," Jane Ann made perfectly clear, "I am returning there to reunite with my husband and son. I'm not going for a visit or a picnic! I am not seeking companionship! I do not need a man to protect me anyway. What I need is a real Guide to show me the right direction. Surely, as the Sheriff here you know of at least one real guide who wants a job!"

The Sheriff looked at George a moment.

George shook his head vigorously. "No, sir," he affirmed, "I have no idea about directions, much less about Indians and fighting. I can hold my own in a disagreement over cards but I am nowhere near being a fighter or a guide!" George did not feel he was being cowardly either.

"This whole conversation is over," Jane Ann said suddenly. "Let's go, George." Then once outside, she told him, "I am not waiting any longer. I'm going to get a ride on one of the wagons that leaves from the Post Office at ten o'clock every day. I was told yesterday that one leaves every morning to go into Indian territories. I can get back to my family by myself!"

George shrugged. She was probably right. He would accompany her to the Station and see her on one of the wagons, and then hope for the best.

CHAPTER 19

It was a mail wagon that Jane Ann found herself riding in back to Sioux territory. Each day a mail wagon went to take mail across to the trading posts and to reach areas where people had started building homes and farms and opening up new towns.

"There are not many towns in the Sioux territory yet," Jane Ann was told by Superintendent Peacock who was riding in the mail wagon with her, "but one day the countryside will be covered with towns and shops and farms all over." Then, in an angry voice, "Of course, the Government is going to have to move the Indians first!"

"Don't you think there is room for both whites and Indians, Mr. Peacock?" Jane asked politely.

"Never!" he practically screamed back, "Never! They are savages, they are not civilized at all. They could not possibly cohabit with the whites." Then he thought a minute and added, "I doubt if they could even be educated enough in three generations to be brought up to the white level. No, no! It just would not work at all." He seemed to have it all figured out.

"I hate to disagree with you, Mr. Peacock, and get off on the wrong foot here," Jane Ann said quietly, "but I was saved from death in an avalanche by the Lakota Sioux over four years ago. My parents died in that avalanche. Ever since then I have lived, excuse me, I meant 'cohabited' with the Indians with no problems at all." She smiled as she watched his lips curl in disgust. "In fact, Mr. Peacock, I am married to a Sioux Indian, and I have a little son named Harry." She watched as his face turned livid and he groped for the right words to say.

"Humph," was all he could muster. It was enough.

There were three drivers with them in the beginning. Each one took over for the other when they stopped and replaced the horses that were pulling them. So, other than changing drivers and horses, the trip was non-stop, except, of course, for personal relief of the two passengers, until they got to the first Trading Post. Jane Ann was anxious to arrive as soon as possible. The second stop would bring them back to the Trading Post near Red Cloud's camp, and this is the stop she waited breathlessly for. Of course, she had not read any of the newspaper articles about the seizure of Red Cloud's camp by the U.S. Cavalry as George had done. She would wonder later why he had not told her about it.

As the wagon pulled to a stop in front of the familiar wooden building, Jane Ann thought about the night the fire had threatened the building and Red Cloud and all the young braves had come out with buckets of water to help put out the fire.

She thought about going inside and confronting the clerk angrily to let him know that she was still alive and had returned to her family. She could even threaten to have him arrested for helping Pierson kidnap her. However, she did none of that. All she wanted was to get across the creek to Red Cloud's camp!

Jane Ann needed more than anything in the world to put her arms around Harry and smell his sweet baby smell. And, of course, to have Bear Claw's arms around her! Then everything in the world would be alright again.

She bought a pony from the driver of the mail wagon, and she paid him twice what it was worth just so she would not have to go inside and face the clerk just yet. She would do that later with Bear Claw or Red Cloud, or even both of them! The men watched her limp over to the horse, but no one offered to help her. She pulled her skirts up to climb and straddle the horse without even a saddle. She guessed some eyebrows were raised at her behavior, but she did not care. She was in a hurry.

As she was riding into Red Cloud's camp, she found it quiet. Many of the tipis had been torn down and removed. At first, as she began to walk around, she wondered if everyone had been moved to another location. She began to change her mind about that though when she began to find evidence of an attack by the Cavalry!

She saw where the ground had been brushed smooth, and where dirt from another area had been brought in and spread out to cover over some places where blood had spilled on the underneath soil. She looked in her tipi and found Harry's puppy. It must have been overlooked by those who cleaned up after the attack. The puppy had been shot and had died cuddling there beside the Indian doll Rena had made for Harry. It was almost out of sight just as if the poor thing had been hiding.

Jane Ann felt intense anger. What kind of people would kill helpless children? Or old women and old men? Surely, she reasoned over and over, Harry and Bear Claw are safe. I cannot lose either of them! The more she walked and looked around the camp, the louder grew her sobs until she was walking around ringing her hands and crooning the Icilowan, the Cherokee death chant. Red Cloud's village was dead! As quick as she thought that, she did not want to think Harry or Bear were dead! "Not my loved ones! Not Harry or Bear. Not Rena or Grandfather. Not Red Cloud. They have to be alive and hiding. But where?

Maybe they were in hiding at one of the decoy camps. But where? The decoy camps had once been a secret joke among the Sioux to throw off their enemies. When they started befriending the Cavalry, they decided they would set up several small camps and then one "REAL" camp, just so the Cavalry would never be sure exactly where to find the chiefs.

Inside her tipi, Jane Ann found some of her drawings. Most of them were gone. "I have to stay calm," she thought. "I know Bear and Harry are fine." But as she walked from one section of the camp to another, from one tipi to another still standing, and found them empty, found them swept clean of their former inhabitants, she wondered.

Then, Jane Ann rode the pony to Sitting Bull's camp and she did not find anyone there either. Slowly all hopes were being put out like candles. Where could she look next? Desperate to find someone, anyone, she began to ride around to all the decoy camps she remembered how to locate, and she found nobody in those camps either. Where would all the people go?

Finally, she headed out to the fort at Laramie. It was getting dark by then but she rode on anyway. She remembered the way Grandfather had told her to watch the landmarks so she would not get lost if she ever went to the fort. But she had never wanted to go there before. She never liked Cavalry, she would never trust them, not after the incident in the Crow camp with the man, Sheffield. She shivered as she remembered him. What if that was the kind of person she would have to talk to about finding her family? "Oh, well," she thought, "I can do it."

Then she suddenly started sobbing as if her heart would break, or was broken. She wondered what Harry had thought when she did not return and hold him and sing to him and feed him. What had Bear thought? Had he been there in the stream looking for rocks all the time and she had not seen him? Where had Bear been? How could she have set out by herself to find Bear and just left her child alone? Oh, yes, she had left Harry with Rena. Dear Rena! What must Rena have thought of Jane Ann not returning? Looking back, wondering like this, Jane Ann felt like a fool, just as she had the time she had run away and the Crow renegades captured her. Foolish!

It was after dark when she reached the gate at Laramie. Jane Ann called out, "Hi Ho! White woman, Jane Ann . . . . " Then she stopped and thought carefully about her name, "Jane Ann Rogers here!" she continued calling out. They opened the gate.

"Get in here, hurry, maam," one of the soldiers called as he took hold of her horse's reins and rushed her through the gate into the compound. "Are you alone out here?" the young soldier asked her.

"Yes," she said, her voice breathless. She noticed then how young the soldier looked.

"Well, maam, unless you are being chased by savages, I would not advise any woman to be out this late all alone. It is bad out here, truly, truly bad." He shook his head while thinking how foolish this woman was, and that some people just do not ever learn.

"I need to speak to your Commander as soon as possible," Jane Ann requested.

"Go on . . ." he paused and looked at her again. Then he called, "Perkins, come and take her over to Major Jeffers." Then to Jane Ann, he said, "Go on, maam, I'll take care of your horse, I'll see that it's done."

She followed the other soldier. Everyone (and there were few) outside in the Compound, looked at her. They were all surprised to see a woman this late at night. They were surprised to see her limping. When Perkins (the soldier leading her) saw she was limping, he apologized. "I didn't notice before. I'm sorry, I didn't realize you were hurt." He reached immediately to pick her up, to help her, but she pushed him away.

"I'm not hurt," she spoke quickly. "My ankle was crushed when I was a child, and I was left with a limp."

He pointed to the door, but it was already opening, and a young officer came out. The soldier introduced himself to her quickly, but he did not know her name.

"I am Jane Ann Rogers," she ~~said quickly~~ REPLIED. "I need your help, sir, as quickly as possible to find my family."

"Come in and have a cup of coffee and tell me more, Miss Rogers." He held the door politely, and he watched her find a chair. The room was lighted by an oil lamp on a big wooden desk. It looked as if the Major must have been looking at the papers spread out under the light.

Then she caught sight of a shadow, and it was obvious then that he had another visitor sitting across the room in the dark. Jane Ann could hear a rocking chair creak as the person slowly rocked back and forth.

"Of course," he said and then motioned for her to sit in the easy chair beside the desk. Someone brought her a steaming cup of coffee and she thanked him.

Major Jeffers," Jane Ann began as she could see the dark outline of the other man watching her intently. I was kidnapped several weeks ago from the trading post near Red Cloud's river camp." For some reason, she felt uneasy talking openly within hearing of a stranger she could not see. She stopped and looked over toward the sound of the creaking rocker.

"Red Cloud's camp, huh?" Major Jeffers repeated. "Go on."

"I don't believe I care to. I would feel much better, Major, if you would introduce me to your other guest." Jane Ann decided she had already said enough.

"Oh, I will, later, I'm sure. This is a personal friend, and we were having a rather delicate conversation before you came. You can meet my friend soon, but first, go ahead with your request." Major Jeffers answered.

Jane Ann had chills going up and down the back of her neck. She felt edgy, as if dangerous things were going to happen any minute. She wished she was not there at that time. However, there was no other way she knew that she could find Harry and Bear alone.

"Anyway, I was kidnapped by a nasty creature from the Trading Post. I was tied up and transported to St Louis where I escaped with the help of an old friend. Then I immediately set out to return here to my family. When I . . . . " Jane Ann was interrupted.

"Where is the man who supposedly kidnapped you, Madame?" Major Jeffers asked her.

"The Sheriff returned him to another territorial prison where he had escaped earlier. I don't know where. I was not told where. I was interested only in having him leave me alone so I could get back here to my family." She wondered why Major Jeffers continued to interrupt her.

"Then what happened?" Major Jeffers waved his hand for her to continue.

"I came back here and found that . . . . " Jane Ann began again but was once again interrupted.

"And, how did you get back here?" A familiar voice asked from the direction of the creaking chair.

Jane Ann could not place that voice at first, and then she remembered, "It is Peacock!" The railroad superintendent. At that, Jane Ann stood up, grabbed the lamp, and walked over to the rocker where he was sitting. "YOU KNOW EXACTLY HOW I GOT HERE!" she said angrily.

"Yes," Peacock jumped up then and stepped backwards as if trying to get away from her. "And I know you are an Indian lover and a traitor to the United States, and . . .". he was not going to take any chance she was going to hit him with that oil lamp. He was backing away from her. Suddenly, he turned and ran out the door.

Major Jeffers howled. The image of the next Governor of the Sioux Territory running away, frightened out of his wits by a tiny woman with a limp, well, it was to be remembered! "Sit down, sit down," he demanded Jane Ann.

"How dare you have that bigot listening to me beg for your help!" Jane Ann's anger made her face red. In the light of the lamp, she thought she must look like a witch with her red hair. Right now though she did not care!

She sat the lamp back on the desk, but she refused to sit down herself, and she began to pound her hand on his desk. "Major Jeffers, where are the people that were in Red Cloud's camp?" She paused to make sure he was listening, and she leaned down closer to look him directly in the eyes. "Listen to me well, my husband and my son were in that camp! I demand you tell me right now where they are!"

Major Jeffers watched her. He admired bravery in anyone. He could tell, even in the dim light of the lamp, that she had cuts on her mouth and bruises all over her face and neck, and on the one hand he had been able to see. He suddenly began to believe her, perhaps she HAD been kidnapped after all!

"Here, sit down, Miss Rogers," he said, his voice calm. "The people in Red Cloud's camp were all moved to the reservation in Oklahoma territory.

"What about Sitting Bull and his people?" She could not imagine Sitting Bull allowing such a thing to happen.

"Sitting Bull is in prison in another location. I will not divulge that information to you right now. Perhaps later. But, if you will tell me the identity of your husband and son, I will locate them for you." Major Jeffers wondered why an English girl came to be with Indians. It would probably make an interesting story.

Sitting Bull in prison! Jane Ann thought about that gentle mystic. "What did Chief Sitting Bull do to be thrown in prison?" Jane demanded and then quickly asked, "Is Red Cloud in prison also?"

Major Jeffers shook his head, dismissing her question with a wave of his hand. "The names, please, tell me the names of who you are looking for."

Jane Ann shook her head, "A Sioux brave called Bear Claw and my child named Harold. We call him Harry." This was an awful nightmare she hoped would be over soon. She stood there watching the Major look through paper after paper as if searching for names. Finally, he shook his head.

"Those names do not appear on our list." He started explaining, "Everyone who was sent to the reservation in Oklahoma territory, plus all the people who were imprisoned and sent North with Sitting Bull and Red Cloud, all the names are listed here. I do not see the names you gave me."

"Have you a list of those who were murdered?" Jane grimly asked.

"No one was murdered," he replied, "not a single person!"

"Well, why is everybody in St. Louis and Boston talking about a whole camp of hundreds of Indians being murdered?" There are articles in every newspaper, and people are talking about it in the streets!"

"I tell you," Major Jeffers repeated, "Not a single soul was murdered." Then he added icily, "There were some who resisted arrest who had to be put to death."

"Put to death! Murdered! What is the difference in a word? I am trying to find my family here, my husband, my son!" Jane Ann screamed.

The man who brought the coffee to her came into the room again.

"We have a difficult job to do, Miss Rogers, I know you wouldn't understand, this is all Government business." Major Jeffers softened his tone some.

"Is it government business to kill babies?" Jane Ann screamed back at him. "Give me your list, I'll look at the names myself!" She reached for the papers, but the Major caught her hand.

"You are obviously upset, and I can see it is not going to be easy for you to . . ."

But, before Major Jeffers could get another word out, Jane Ann shoved him out of the way and she looked closely to read the names.

He had second thoughts. He decided to just stand there and let her look. He waved the Sergeant away and shook his head to let him know it was alright. Major Jeffers let her look as long as she wanted to, and finally she had seen enough.

"I do not see any of my family listed here." She whispered hoarsely. "None of them." She sighed deeply as if all the fight had suddenly gone out of her. "Does this mean they did not survive the attack on Red Cloud's camp?" She walked over to him and stood there looking into his eyes. "Does it, sir?"

He didn't answer her at first. He was having a hard time enough with the whole incident and now this woman comes in here looking for a husband and a baby. There were children killed in the raid. There were men and women and old people killed. Major Jeffers had been afraid of the Sioux when he first rode in there with his men looking for Chief Red Cloud. The order had been to hold their fire, but some young cavalry recruit who had never laid eyes on an Indian before got scared and started shooting. One shot led to many, and every man got jittery, and nobody knew who was directing the shooting. He had watched in horror as unarmed people were slaughtered. It was something he never wanted to talk about to anyone. In fact, he was determined to lie about it as often as possible. As it turned out, the Chief was not even in the village. They had to hunt him down somewhere else.

"I don't know what to say to you," Major Jeffers told Jane Ann. "There is no list of the dead, if that's what you mean. We could not identify them. We buried them decently, that's about all we could do."

Jane Ann suddenly heard herself screaming and quite without warning, she fell to the floor in a dead faint.

CHAPTER 20

Jane Ann woke up lying in a feather bed under the covers dressed in a woman's nightgown. She was amazed to see on the walls all around the room her own drawings. Some of them were framed, some were without frames. It was an amazing experience to open her eyes and see Harry, Grandfather, Rena, Red Cloud, Rain, all the people she had loved so very long now looking down at her sleeping in a white man's bed!

Immediately she jumped up and began to look for her clothes. They were nowhere. She opened the door and walked out into a room filled with soldiers. There was a lot of polite coughing and turning of heads. She looked around the faces desperately trying to find Major Jeffers when suddenly the door to the outside opened and in walked the Major with the man, Peacock, from the railroad.

Jeffers smiled and took off his hat and bowed.

Jane Ann knew he was mocking her.

Peacock looked away as if embarrassed.

The others in the room began to move around, began acting as if they were busy working.

Jane Ann was flustered, but she remembered to say firmly, "I'll thank you for my clothes immediately!" This seemed to cause a lot of throat clearing and chuckles around the room. Then she turned and walked back in the bedroom and slammed the door.

Someone brought her clothes all clean and ready to put on. Someone brought a tray of food with hot steaming tea and a note that said, "Sorry, maam, I didn't realize you were English last night. Excuse the coffee." She did not find it amusing.

She ate bites even as she was remembering how it felt to hold Harry. First thing in the morning was cuddle time for them, and she would hold him for hours. Also, she would carry him everywhere with her all day long without ever getting tired. She even changed his clothes while carrying him. That is until Bear Claw teased her about his legs becoming crooked because of not standing and running and walking. She had known what it was not to be able to walk or run for so very long.

It was while she was remembering that she suddenly saw the drawing of Bear Claw directly in front of her. She looked at the thatch of red curls tied tight in his black shiny hair and a pain shot through her middle. His strong hands were on his knees in the drawing, but she could remember them holding her, gently touching her. Tears streamed again down her face. She wondered if she would ever find Harry, or find Bear Claw, or find anyone.

"Oh, God," Jane Ann prayed, "If ever you let White Buffalo Woman tell me a truth before, please let her tell me now where Harry and Bear are. Please! Please!" She was whispering when Major Jeffers opened the door.

"I trust you had a restful night," he said pleasantly enough, "and I imagine you enjoyed waking with your family all around you."

"I don't know," Jane Ann answered coldly, "I don't care whether you are being sly or sincere, I'm through playing games, I'm through asking you anything. I just have one more question, Major Jeffers."

He looked at her tear stained face and noticed how lovely, how vulnerable she was, and he wondered if this were his sister, his wife, how differently he would feel. He nodded.

"Am I to be sent to a reservation also?" Jane Ann's voice was cold, icy, "If not, and if you continue to refuse to tell me where my husband and my son are, I will leave."

Major Jeffers applauded the woman's courage again in his mind. She must have gone through a lot lately. Peacock had said she told the same thing about being abducted while she was at the station and on the wagon riding back from St. Louis with him. He and the Sergeant had changed her clothes because there was no other woman on post at the time. He had felt her comfort required it. They were both ashamed, however, when they found all the bruises and marks. They both knew she had not been lying. Someone had kidnapped her. Someone had beat her! Yet, none of that had stopped her from coming back for her baby and her husband! Even after he had practically admitted to her they were dead, she still persisted! He wished for a moment, half his men had her courage. There would be no place for fear for any of them! He shook his head.

"I cannot tell you what I do not know," he answered gently.

She got up from her chair and started out the door.

"Wait, Miss Rogers, wait and I will have your drawings taken down," the Major called.

"No need," Jane Ann said as she kept walking, slowly, limping until she was out the door. Once outside, she batted her eyes against the sun. It was a very bright day. She vowed not to let the sun go down until she had Harry in her arms. And herself in Bear's arms.

Someone brought her pony to her. The lieutenant thought it best not to let the girl limp across the courtyard with everybody in sight, because they all were feeling sorry for her already. They watched her ride out. Once outside the fort, Jane Ann gave the pony his reins and they galloped furiously toward Sitting Bull's decoy camp high in the Black Hills.

She allowed the horse periods of rest and plenty of water and grass, but she hurried him, kept him galloping as long as she could. Finally they were there. The familiar Black Hills came into sight long before they drew near. It was almost dark again when she pulled her pony into a turn and walked him down into the ravine. It was a secret place high in the hills that few people knew about. The only reason she had known about it was Sitting Bull. He had told her one time in a teasing voice that White Buffalo Woman would probably tell her anyway, so he better go ahead and tell her first. That's when he brought Jane riding up into the hills and surprised her with the sharp down turn into the ravine, a hidden ravine where caves lined the wall and ancient drawings decorated them all. A secret place she had slipped off to and visited more often than she could count.

"Oh, God, if only I can find them here." At first, all she heard was total silence. No sounds at all. She knew that was impossible. The animals would not stop walking about, crawling around on the tree lined floor of the ravine, and they would make their usual grunting noises. Yet the animals were quiet. She knew that meant others were here and she was determined to find them. But it was pitch dark!

Jane Ann sat out in the open as close to the center of the ravine as she could judge in the dark. She sat with her legs folded under and with her eyes closed. She was not going to move until she had them all back!

There she sat a long time waiting, hoping, praying, believing. Then, finally, in the darkness, a hand gently pressed down on her shoulder, and a voice whispered in the stillness, "Jane Ann, welcome home."

She turned and was lifted gently to her feet. She could see only by the dimmest of the moon's light that Rain was there. She could see no one else, hear no one else. Rena and Grandfather, Rain, dear Rain, who had been the first to touch her frozen crushed foot under the snow. She stood, with her tears streaming, holding to him, not daring to speak aloud, waiting for the other hands to reach for her, waiting for her baby's soft body to be pressed close to hers, waiting . . . .

Then, without warning, Rain choked and, letting her go, he fell back. From his lips came the most awful scream Jane Ann had ever heard. It was a combination of a mourning cry and a cry of pain mixed with an angry piercing yell that said nothing but yet it split the air with its agony.

She fell on him, feeling his face, his mouth, not wanting him to die, wanting him to speak, to tell her where their people were, to give her back their happy days. Even as she was pleading with him not to die, she knew he had already gone. That terrible cry was his spirit leaving his body.

She sat there holding his head in her lap hours and hours waiting for the dawn to come, waiting for light so she could look at him, so she could tell him how grateful she was for her own life. Maybe he was just hurt. Maybe he would wake up when the sun rose into view. Maybe. Hours of tears left her face dry and tight. It was hard to open and close her eyes. They felt like sharp rocks rubbing beneath her eyelids. Several times she tried to pray aloud, to sing softly, but her voice was too strained.

Just as the sun was rising, she called out with a piercing scream that rent the air. She heard herself making the yodel sound that all the Indians could make easily, that she had never been able to do, something with her tongue in her throat like Rena had shown her, but which Jane had never mastered. Now at dawn it shot out of her like a call to all of nature. She looked down into the agonizing face of her friend, her brother, Rain. He was dead, little bubbles of blood seeped from his lips. She sat for a long time looking at him. Then she began singing her admiration of him, of how brave a warrior he was, of what a good brother and friend he was. She sang softly all day long until it was night again, and she could no longer see his face, no longer see the sun.

Later, the next morning, she knew White Buffalo Woman was walking there in the ravine helping her pick up enough wood to make a funeral bier. Helping her pick up Rain's body and put it high in the air as befits a warrior. Up there the Spirits would see him and hear his spirit heart, and they would come take his spirit and give his body to the eagles and the hawks.

Jane Ann and White Buffalo Woman chanted the Icilowan, the Sioux death song. Over and over they repeated it. Jane Ann called for the Spirits and cried out loud over and over. Then White Buffalo Woman pointed to the horizon. There before Jane Ann stood Rain with his arm outstretched to her. For a minute, she thought the past hours and days had been a dream, that this was real, that Rain was not dead but wanted her to come with him. He did not speak to her though. Instead, she heard a mournful whisper.

"Go home, Jane Ann, show people who we really are." Rain called to her from the Spirit world. White Buffalo Woman called to her from the Spirit world. Many spirits called and sang to her from the Spirit world. She looked and kept looking. She would not leave yet. Then White Buffalo Woman stepped aside and waved Jane Ann to look farther; and there before her, playing in a meadow filled with brightly colored flowers and many bright butterflies, there ran Harry and Bear together.

Jane Ann immediately stood to run toward them, but Rain whispered, "No" and "Go home, Jane Ann, show who we really are." White Buffalo Woman said also, "Go, Jane Ann." Jane crumpled to the ground and lay sobbing and screaming until all her tears were spent. Until she could feel the cool air of coming evening again. Until some Great Spirit that loved her very much caused her to sleep and sleep and sleep. Then, finally, Jane Ann lifted herself up and pulled her pony's reins.

"You've rested long enough," she said softly to her pony while she was taking the cavalry saddle off. She intended to ride out of there like a Sioux woman, proud and free. She intended to draw the faces of her beloved people over and over until everyone in the whole world looked into their eyes. Until everyone knew them as she did!

CHAPTER 21

Jane Ann saw Uncle Percy and Aunt Agnes even before they saw her. She waved and waved until Uncle Percy leaned and pointing up to where Jane Ann was, he told Agnes to "Look there!" A big smile covered both their faces.

Jane Ann was filled with a mix of emotions! She thought of Papa and Mama. She finally made it half way down off the ship when strong hands grabbed her and she heard, "Well, it's about time you come home!" She looked up to see Jeremy who picked her up and walked sure footedly down the boardwalk to where Percy and Agnes were waiting. Jane Ann thought she could see tears in his eyes. She whispered "I'm so glad to see you, Jeremy. Thank you!" He let her go only so Dr. Rogers and Mrs. Rogers could welcome her.

They took turns welcoming her home. Aunt Agnes whispered in her ear, "We are so glad to see you, Jane Ann!." She kissed her cheek.

Percy leaned and looked at her with tears in his eyes. "Welcome home, Jane Ann, the years have been long." She moved closer into his arms and she heard him clear his throat and then whisper, "I am overwhelmed . . . . I have so much to say to you . . . . oh, it is so good to see you, my girl." Later, at home, he intended to tell her what he should have long ago. And, he had her mother (Dorothy's) diary for her.

Within three weeks, Jane Ann had returned to her adopted parents' home in the Country outside London. Petrie and Grace were delighted to have her back home, and they were devastated to hear about Harold and Emma dying in an avalanche.

"I was married for almost two years to a Sioux Indian named Bear." Jane Ann told them. "We had a baby son named Harry." She said it quietly. "Would you like to see a painting I did of them together?" She asked in her soft voice. Then she said, "They were both killed by the Cavalry." She didn't tell them she had found their spirits in the sacred Black Hills and that she was allowed to say goodbye to them and their Lakota friends.

"Yes, Ms Jane Ann." Grace had answered quietly. It broke her heart to know that Ms. Emma would never rock her grandson, and Ms. Jane would never see him grow to be a man.

Petrie opened the door and followed her through the hallway to her bedroom where he waited at the doorway to take the painting from her and take it to the sitting room where he and Grace could both see it.

Then Jane Ann lifted the cloth to reveal a handsome man with dark eyes and hair to his shoulders sitting beside a young boy who appeared to be about two years old. The boy had red hair like Jane Ann's. Anyone could tell they were father and son by the way the boy leaned against his shoulder in a familiar way.

An article on the front page of the London Daily Express Newspaper March 12, 1867, reads as follows:

> JANE ANN ROGERS is showing portraits and drawings at the London Museum of Art April 21, 1867. Come see the Lakota Sioux of America as Miss Rogers knows them. She lived in the Indian Territories of Western United States and was married to a warrior named Bear. They had a son named Harry. Both Father and Son were killed by the American Cavalry in March 1855. She returned to England and since then she has been showing her paintings in Art Exhibits in Paris, Rome, and Madrid. You are invited to also view this exciting new artist's paintings at the London Bank Downtown. She has been called the FINEST ENGLISH ARTIST of the Nineteenth Century.